APPLE BLOSSOMS IN MONTANA

ORCHARD BRIDES SERIES BOOK 6

LUCINDA RACE

MC TWO PRESS

Editor Susan of West of Mars
Proofreader Kimberly Dawn

Cover design by Jade Webb www.meetcutecreative.com

Manufactured in the United States of America
First Edition June 2022

Print Edition ISBN 978-1-954520-29-5
E-book ISBN 978-1-954520-28-8

AUTHOR'S NOTE

Hi and welcome to my world of romance with a touch of magic. I hope you love with my characters as much I do. So, turn the page and fall in love again.

If you'd like to stay in touch, please join my Newsletter. I release it twice per month with tidbits, recipes and an occasional special gift just for my readers so sign up here: https://lucindarace.com/newsletter/ and there's a free book when you join!

Happy reading...

$\mathcal{R}$enee Mitchell couldn't believe her eyes. The small apple trees that had taken her days to plant were trampled into the ground and the culprits were grazing on the new shoots of grass between what was to be the new section in her orchard. She threw her head back and let out an ear-splitting scream. That helped her feel a smidge better, not that anyone could hear her since this was Big Sky Country, Montana, where every day of the growing season was critical. If she could even get new stock, it would be at least a two-week setback and she was not calling her parents in New Mexico to share the bad news. Riverbank Orchard was her business now and she'd figure out a solution on her own. But first these stupid cows needed to get off her land before they did even more damage.

Cautiously, she inched closer to the large beasts, wary of how they might react. At least they didn't have those wide horns that were famous in Texas. All these cows had were yellow tags dangling like earrings from their ears. Maybe it had the name of the ranch stamped on them.

Once she got close enough without spooking one, she discovered they were numbers only. She popped her hands on her hips. "That's not going to do me a bit of good."

She reached for her cell phone but didn't bother pulling it out. Cell reception was spotty out here, and besides, who was she going to call with her tale of woe? It's not like there was a local resource to help find lost cattle, was there?

In the distance, on the other side of the small riverbed, she could see a lone figure galloping in her direction. Maybe that was the person responsible for these beasts. She stomped through the now downed trees, closing the distance between herself and the horse and rider. A man was in the saddle, and as they got closer, she could tell he was tall but not who he was. His cowboy hat was pulled low over his face, probably to keep the bright sun from his eyes, or more likely to not see the mess his cows made to her field. For a fraction of a second she thought about the fence she should have put up first, but once the cows were out of the barn, there was no use worrying about the door being closed.

She lifted a hand in greeting and called out to him. "Missing any cows?"

He pulled up on the reins and came to a full stop on the opposite side of the river. He scanned the landscape in back of her and scowled. "As a matter of fact, I am and I can see they've invaded your orchard."

There was something about the man that was vaguely familiar, and his smooth voice tickled a long-ago memory, but Renee dismissed it. She needed to stick to the business at hand and have him move his cows back across the river. If they crossed once, they could do it again; the water wasn't that high or running too fast now that the spring thaw was over for the most part.

"Well, we're going to need to discuss the damage they did."

The man urged his horse through the stream, and it danced up the low-rise bank in front of her. He swung his leg over the saddle and jumped down before giving her a hard look. A flicker of recognition flashed in his caramel-brown eyes, but it was gone just as quickly. Clearly, they must have met, and then Renee knew. She took a step back and stumbled. Before she landed on her butt, he had reached out and steadied her.

"Renee, are you alright?"

The deep timbre of his voice caused her heart to skip. Hank Shepard. The first boy she had ever kissed and the one man she had never forgotten. It had been almost twenty years since she had seen him and other than a touch of gray in his light-brown hair and the sun crinkles around his eyes, he looked exactly the same—drop-dead gorgeous as ever. It would have been better if he'd gotten out of shape with a big belly but no, he had stayed trim and muscular. And this was all with a quick assessment.

"Renee?"

Despite the way his voice made her belly flip, she had to focus on the question and not the man asking it.

"Yes, I'm fine. I just tripped on a root."

He looked down at the grassy bank and gave her a quirk of a smile. "Glad it wasn't anything bigger."

She wanted to groan but there wasn't much else to say about the invisible root. "So, about your cows." She couldn't help but notice he still held her arm in his hand and she took a step back to break the connection so she could think clearly.

"There not really mine, more like my parents'. I'm home helping out while Dad recovers from a broken hip, you know, kinda running things for him. Then I'll head back to Dallas. I'm a lawyer now."

It was funny how he slipped that in, and there went the idea of suing the cows for damages. She laughed—suing cows.

"What's funny, me being a lawyer or living in Dallas?" He gave her a long look just like he did when they were kids and he was trying to figure out what she was thinking.

"It's nothing other than we need to talk about the damage done to my orchard. I just planted new tree stock last week and now your cows"—she pointed over her shoulder—"your dad's cows used them like they were the yellow brick road."

"It might not be that bad; do you mind if I take a look?"

She swept her hand in the direction of the field. "See for yourself."

He looked from side to side. "Where's the fencing?"

She kicked the ground with the toe of her work boot. "On order. It should be here in a few days." Which was the least of her problems. Once it was delivered, she didn't know how she'd hire anyone to help her get it installed. She had resigned herself to setting posts herself. She was more than capable given that she had done it a bunch of times with Dad years ago. It was like muscle memory; the know-how would just come back to her.

If he sensed she was holding anything back, he didn't show it. With a curt nod, he said, "Care to lead the way?"

With his horse walking behind him, Hank followed Renee as she crossed the section of field that hadn't been planted, at least not this year, and she wanted to cry when she saw the tiny green leaves crushed into the rows of dirt and the brown sticks split like strands of spaghetti noodles. The analogy was the best she could up with and since pasta was her least favorite food, it was okay to compare the damage to Italian food.

"Renee, I'm really sorry about the mess. Get me the cost estimate of the damage and I'll cut you a check so you can buy new trees."

That was nice of him but he didn't understand; it wasn't just the tree stock. She'd need to turn over the soil again, prep the bare root stock, and replant. She was looking at a couple more weeks of work and then the fence on top of that.

"I can do that." She looked at the cows munching on what was left of her field, and not that she was counting, but there had to be at least fifty of them. On the upside, any cow patties left behind were free fertilizer, but who was she kidding. That wasn't much of a consolation prize.

He pulled his billfold out of his front jeans pocket and handed her a business card. "My email address is on there so just send it over and I'll drop off a check tomorrow if that's okay."

"Yeah, sure. I'll probably be out here so you can just leave it in the mailbox." She'd have to hook up the plow to get the rows churned up again. But at least she could get the stock on order and the land would be ready when it arrived. Then again, maybe she could expedite the shipment too; after all, how much could that cost?

She gave Hank a steady look. Maybe she'd just slide the air freight charges into the price of the trees so he'd have to pay for it. But she quickly dismissed that idea. That was dishonest, and they had been friends once upon a time. She wouldn't do that to an enemy, let alone an old friend.

He gave her that wide smile that she remembered so well and her stomach was like a bunch of honey bees buzzing around the buttercups in spring.

"I'll drive these girls across the river, and I'll swing by tomorrow so don't forget to email me. And I'm real sorry about all of this, but you should get the fence installed before you plant again."

Yeah, yeah, yeah, she should do a lot of things and if she ever got to that to-do list she wrote out for herself, she'd be organized and already prepared for fall harvest. As it was, she hadn't even had time to turn the list over and start with what she had thought was the number one priority. Not that she'd admit any of this to Hank, but as far as he was concerned, she was the businesswoman of the year in River Junction—well, maybe the orchard businesswoman of the year at a bare minimum.

She forced a bright smile. "It's at the top of my list."

"Good." He stuck his left boot in the stirrup and settled into the saddle like he'd been born to be a cowboy. She thought it was ironic since that was what he'd been born into and now it seemed he turned in his Wranglers and Stetson for a suit and tie.

He gave a sharp whistle, and the cows slowly raised their heads while he maneuvered his horse through the herd. Once he got to the farthest bunch, he began to herd them in her direction. She moved off to one side and was surprised to see it looked like he had been doing this forever, instead of leaving Montana after high school graduation, never to return except for quick holiday trips.

But who was she to judge? Hadn't she done the same thing? College and then worked in a city? At least her plan had always been to make money so that someday she'd return home and run the family orchard. Once, when they were young, Hank said when he left, he wasn't ever living in small town USA again.

As he rode past her, he tipped his hat and winked. "See you tomorrow, Renee, and by the way, you're looking pretty as always." He tapped his spurs into the sides of his horse and finished driving the herd to the edge of the water before splashing across.

She watched until Hank and the cows were out of sight, heading back toward the Shepard Ranch. She had to wonder how long he would be in town. Maybe they could get together for coffee or something, just for old times' sake, of course. She crossed the dirt path where her bicycle was leaning against a fence post. She'd best get back to the house and dig up the paperwork and then source new tree stock and place the order. She was counting on these new apple trees to be producing in a couple of years. If she was going to make a viable business of the orchard, she needed to expand and produce a line of products made from apples to sell at tourist stores all across the state. And if that went well, she was thinking of what other kinds of trees she could plant and expand the business even more.

She took one last look over her shoulder and could see the orchard in her mind's eye, lush with flowers budding with apples, glorious apples. There was nothing like Montana in the spring.

2

---

*H*ank couldn't believe his luck; he just ran into Renee. He turned in the saddle to catch one last glimpse of her. It had been years since he had laid eyes on the one girl who had stolen his heart when they were in middle school, and he wasn't sure about the mixed-up feelings and emotions that bubbled up inside of him all from being close to her.

The lowing cattle drew his attention away from thoughts of Renee, but he was surprised to discover he wanted to talk with her longer. Wanting to help her after his family's cattle destroyed all her new trees was his second reaction after his first was to take her in his arms and kiss her just to see if the old flame was still there. His cows trampled her crop; the least he could do was to purchase new stock and find a way to help her replant. By the looks of the empty field, she was the only one working today.

He'd ask Dad about her situation as soon as he got back to the house because his pop always had the pulse on the happenings in River Junction. After the cows were secured in the paddock, he rode the fence line to discover where it was down. It was not going to work if the cows kept breaking out now that they found fresh grass and an easy way to get to the other side of the river. With a snort, he thought, *Maybe the grass was greener on the other side.*

As he rode back to the barn, he kept an eye out, looking for Louie, the ranch foreman. Hank gave a sharp whistle and he started walking toward him. After he filled Louie in on the problem, he confirmed some of the ranch hands would get out in the south pasture and get the fence repaired.

"Hey, Dad," he called as he walked into the house and headed to his dad's favorite place since he had surgery for his broken hip, his man cave, also known as the den.

"Hank, back here."

He entered the room and Dad was relaxing in his recliner, the walker within arm's reach. Dad set his book aside and gave Hank a welcoming smile. It was like looking into the future by thirty years; they had the same smile, dimple, and eyes.

"Dad, around fifty head of our cattle got out and found their way across that small river, you know the one that's out past the south pasture. Well, they crossed into Riverbank Orchard and had a field day."

He frowned. "That doesn't sound good; did they do any damage?"

Not that he thought the neighbors would sue them but maybe he should have taken pictures with his cell phone to show Dad. "Do you know if Renee Mitchell is running the place now? I didn't see her dad around when I was over there."

"Yeah, she took over last fall. I heard something about her parents moving to Arizona or New Mexico, taking a break for a bit from farm life, but you know, nobody ever really gets tired of Montana. It's in their blood, and I'll bet they'll be back this summer to help Renee. Did she say if she's got the same crew over there for that orchard?"

"What are you talking about?" Most people didn't change jobs like the wind around here. When you found a good job, you hung on to it, and you either fell in love with the area or you didn't. There were no two ways about it.

"I guess you didn't hear; they've had some tough times. I'm guessing that's why she moved back from Chicago. Your mom said she was some big shot interior designer. And then two years ago, they lost their crop to a late snowstorm. That's hard for any farmer and it doesn't matter if you're raising cows or chickens or vegetables and fruits, bad weather never helps your bottom line."

"Yeah, I know that we've had many a tough year here, Dad, but somehow you always manage to find a way to make it work."

Mom walked into the room and handed him a mug and small plate. The coffee teased his nose, but the cookies made his mouth water. This was something he'd missed, his favorite chocolate chip cookie. If he had one weakness, it'd be cookies with chunks of dark chocolate. "Thanks, Mom, but I would have gotten up."

"It wasn't any bother. I was bringing some in to your dad, and this way I get you to stay for a few minutes and fill me in on what's been going on before you get busy again. I know there are a lot of hours still left in the day and you won't be back until suppertime."

"Mom, you definitely know how to spoil your favorite son."

"It's a good thing your brother is out of town; he'd be wrestling you for those cookies."

Dad cleared his throat. "Maeve, we were just talking about Riverbend Orchard."

"Is that your way of asking me to pipe down for a few minutes?"

He blew her a kiss. "You know me so well, but anyway, Hank, ranching is different than farming. Apple blossoms are fragile like newborn babies and without that beginning step, there isn't a harvest and there's nothing you can do about Mother Nature."

"Yeah, you've been saying that all my life, but our cows damaged all her new root stock so I'm going to buy new, and for the record, I'm not expecting it to come out of the ranch budget. Renee needs help and I intend on helping her."

"Son, you're a good man and I wouldn't expect anything else, but is it more than just being neighborly? Did any of those old feelings surface when you saw her again?"

Mom was watching this exchange with keen interest even if she hadn't interjected yet. It was her way to let Dad do most of the talking, not that she didn't have an opinion because she always did. Out of the corner of his eye, he noticed she sat up straighter in the chair and leaned forward.

"Now, I'm not sure there was a twinge, but it was nice to see her. And even though we dated years ago, I'm sure there's not much left to resurrect, and besides, Renee has probably long since moved on." Who was he trying to convince, his parents or himself? There was a part of his heart that did feel the pull.

Dad dunked his cookie in his coffee. "Well, I happen to

know she's single." He looked at Hank over the rim of the mug and winked.

So now he understood where this was going. Dad was playing matchmaker. "That doesn't mean I can hang around River Junction. I have a thriving law practice in Dallas."

"You do, but you know what they say, son; once Montana gets in your blood, it never leaves."

Dad stopped talking as Mom slowly shook her head.

Hank knew Montana was a part of him and there was something about this land and this ranch that caused his heart to beat at a slow and steady pace the minute he drove under the wooden arch. But he had a life in Dallas. How was he supposed to pick up and move back to the ranch and throw away all those years of law school? It wasn't like he could practice law here since there wasn't much call for a defense attorney out of these parts.

"Thanks for the reminder, Dad." He settled back in a comfortable armchair.

Dad looked up from his coffee cup and gave him a sharp look. "Son, do you know where the cattle crossed the stream?"

"Yes, and Louie already sent some of the hands out to fix it. But it wasn't just that they got on her land, but that they trampled her freshly planted trees and they couldn't have been more than three feet tall. You know what a nine-hundred-plus-pound cow can do to land when they graze."

"Yeah, you're right." He turned to his wife. "Let your mother know how much it costs to replace the trees and we'll take the money out of our account to pay for them. It's not right that you have to pay for it out of your money; we can afford it. We're doing just fine, and besides, neighbors help neighbors around here and it's not just about helping other cattle folk. Farms are just as important to our area."

His dad and mom were hard-working people and they had their share of rough times, but they had always found a way to help their friends and neighbors.

"Well, I'm gonna head out. Thanks for the shot of caffeine and sugar, Mom. I'm going to check to make sure that fence is fixed. I'll see you at dinner." He stood, then picked up his hat, but didn't place it on his head. "Louis is going to need another pair of hands to move the cows once the fence is mended and I want to make sure they don't find their way back across the stream tomorrow."

"What about the rest of the fencing?"

Dad worked his way to the edge of his chair and dragged his walker over to him. He heaved himself up with a grunt. Hank watched as he swayed from side to side before he settled in and continued, at the ready to lend a hand if needed, but Dad had his pride and Hank needed to wait.

"I'll make sure a couple of the ranch hands inspect the entire fence line. It'll take a while, but again, we need to keep our neighbors safe. Besides, that river's fast in spots and we don't wanna lose any of the herd."

He gave a sharp nod. "I'll look forward to what you find out."

Mom was now standing next to her husband, her arm resting on his. "Dear, you should be taking it easy."

"I'm bored to tears and if there was a way I could get on a horse, I'd be out there riding the fence line, if nothing else than for a change of scenery."

"I'll take some pictures, Dad, so you'll be in the loop."

He patted Hank's shoulder. "In case I forgot to tell you,

I really appreciate you coming home to help out. I see the doctor next week and hopefully he'll release me back to work."

"Don't push it, Dad. I'll stay as long as you need."

*L*ater that night, after dinner and a hot shower, Hank checked his email. There was one from Riverbend Orchard. He smiled and scanned the contents and then went back to read it again before looking at the attachment. Renee was nothing if not thorough. She attached a scan of the invoice where she had made notations of the extra fertilizer she used and what she needed for other enhancements to give the trees a boost but there's nothing in here about labor hours to plant. He knew it was gonna cost her overtime for people to replant. It was curious she hadn't written that down too.

Tomorrow when he took the check over, he'd ask about the labor and see if there was something more he could do to help her. Dad had taught him to always pay it forward, help out your neighbors, but in this case, it was more than that. He wanted to help out an old friend.

He sat back in the chair and looked out the window as shadows lengthened across the ranch. Was there something more like Dad had implied? They'd been best friends and then high school sweethearts. They'd agreed to keep in touch when they went off to different colleges and at first they had, but by the time holiday break rolled around, they had drifted apart. With a shake of his head, he told himself this was all because he still considered her a good friend.

3

Renee sat on the tractor, hands resting on the wheel, shoulders slumped, facing the task before her. She was annoyed it had to be done at all. With a flick of the gear switch, she lowered the plow into the dark, almost black, soil. Defeat washed over her as she put the tractor in low gear and began to plow the first long row and down the next, making slow progress.

As she drove, her thoughts turned to inspecting the current root stock, hoping some could be saved but a scant twenty trees were not going to breathe new life into her orchard. She toiled under the warm spring sun for the next two hours, plowing the earth row after row, moving at a slow and steady pace. She wasn't able to bring on any extra workers today to help because she was already over budget with this project and every penny counted.

By midmorning she needed to take a break. She crossed the gravel drive with a heavy heart and once inside the old farmhouse, she poured herself a large glass of ice-cold water from the pitcher in the icebox. Did anyone even call it an icebox anymore? she wondered.

Today the quiet was unnerving; she wished she had someone to talk to about what she was facing—not to solve her problems but as a sounding board. Her old kitty, Smokey, pretty much slept all the time and he was no help.

As she finished her water, a pickup truck parked up next to the house. The truck bore the logo Stone Throw Ranch. What was going on? She put the glass on the sideboard and went out to the back porch. Lo and behold, there was Hank Shepard, looking handsome as ever with that swagger in his walk. He raised his hand in greeting and gave her that familiar, heart-fluttering smile.

"Morning, Renee." He reached the stairs, and putting one foot on the lower step, he leaned toward her. "What's the good word this morning?"

"Oh, you know, just working. Farming life is a lot like ranching. Get up with the sun, work, work, and more work. Take a break, then work some more, break for lunch, and repeat for the afternoon." She hoped her voice didn't sound as weary as she felt. The last thing she needed was him to feel sorry for her.

He handed her an envelope, a nondescript ordinary envelope which she figured held the check. But her heart sank a little. The money would help but how was she going to get the new tree stock here fast? When she checked online, it was back-ordered for a month. She forced a tight smile. "Thanks, I appreciate the help."

"You're welcome but it was our cattle who trampled your trees and made a mess of your field so it's the least we can do to help. And if your apples had made a mess of my cattle, heck, I'd be expecting some sort of payment in return."

"Thanks. You always knew how to take something and twist it around to your advantage." What she didn't say was he always knew how to make her laugh and that hadn't changed. "I'll make sure to keep my unruly apples out of your field."

Now he really chuckled, a deep unrestrained kind of laugh. "Heck, the cows would love your apples; they'd be like sweet, delicious, juicy treats for them. After all, look how much they enjoyed the trees."

She thought he'd send over the check and not come himself so why was he standing here making small talk? She had a ton of work to do. But she wasn't going to get snarky with him; after all, he did pay for the damage.

He casually looked around and if he noticed there weren't any vehicles in the parking area, he didn't acknowledge it. For a few moments she wanted to hand the envelope back to him, but that was her pride talking and it would be foolish. As much as she hated to take the money, she knew she had no other choice; another bank loan wasn't an option either.

"I appreciate you stopping over and let your parents know this fall, apples are on me."

He straightened up. "I'll be sure to tell them, and you know, Renee, I was thinking." He looked at his watch and back to her.

"Uh-oh. If I remember correctly, that was never a good sign when we were kids, the *I was thinking* phrase." She held his gaze, her eyes locked on his.

"No, this is good." He held up the Boy Scout salute. "Promise." He pointed to the envelope. "Why don't you open that."

"I'll do that later. I really need to get back to work."

He looked in the direction of the tractor. "Plowing up the rows?"

Now he was starting to irritate her. She didn't have

time to be jaw jacking when there was plowing to do. She crossed her arms over her midsection and scuffed the toe of her boot against the porch floor.

"Do me a favor and open the envelope."

She hated when anyone pushed her to do something, but if it would get him off her land quicker, she might just as well. She ripped open one end and a paper fluttered to the ground. She picked it up. It wasn't a check.

She could feel the color drain from her face. It was an IOU. How was she going to buy tree stock? She had ten acres to get planted, half of which the cows had destroyed, but she only had enough remaining stock for the five.

"I don't understand." She blinked away any tears that wanted to fall. There was no crying in farming, at least not in front of an old boyfriend.

"When I looked over what you needed to reorder last night, I checked several nurseries online that were similar to where you purchased the original order and they're all sold out for at least a month."

Her temper began to spike. How dare he nose around her business; she hadn't asked him to do anything like that.

"Not to worry, I'll find replacement stock. I have some feelers out and I should have something by the weekend."

He gave her that heart-melting smile again. She was annoyed to discover her heart hadn't crusted over from the pain of losing him and it still caused her to give him a chance.

"That's what I wanted to tell you. I found semi-dwarf tree stock and it will deliver this afternoon. They're all bought and paid for too."

"Hank." Why hadn't he discussed this with her first? Her parents had always planted full-size trees; how would that work? "There are different requirements for how many trees per acre between different sizes."

"Renee, I did the research and I ordered enough for a little over three acres. It was all the supplier had, but he's trying to get more."

"How did you even know the acreage I'm planting?"

He shifted from one foot to the other and grinned. "You make great margin notes. All I had to do was remember your special shorthand and placing the order was a snap."

Her heart constricted. That was a sweet gesture. "You didn't need to go to all the trouble." If she didn't have residual feelings from their childhood, this would have turned the tide in his favor. He was still the good guy she remembered even if he broke her heart—or to be fair, maybe they had broken each other's.

He touched the brim of this tattered high school baseball cap and with a twinkle in his eye, he said, "No trouble at all, ma'am."

Now she couldn't help but let out a good belly laugh. "The Texas drawl does suit you."

"Thank ya kindly. Now if you wouldn't mind a little help, I'd be more than willing to plant a few trees after they arrive."

She could tell her smile faded as his matched hers. "I'm fine, Hank. I've got some good people to help me." The lie died on her lips. The people she hired moved from job to job. They'd always come back, but she had to think about her budget. And if she could get the trees in starting tomorrow, she had to get the plowing done today. With a little luck she'd be finished by suppertime.

He looked around but didn't call her on the bluff. "It's

a standing offer and I've got time to help. So, don't hesitate to ask."

"I appreciate that. I'll let you know when the truck arrives and after I inventory the trees, just to let you know everything's all set."

He took one last look around. "Then I'll head back over to the ranch and maybe we could grab a cup of coffee and a slice of pie at The Filler Up Diner. Mom said Maggie still makes one heck of a pie, even if it's not huckleberry season."

She longed to say yes as fast as the words would come out of her mouth but instead, she said, "Maybe."

His smile didn't fade. "See you around, Renee, and remember to call if you need anything."

"Thanks, Hank, and tell your mom and dad I said hello."

A wave of loneliness swept over her as he got in his truck and did a wide turn in the middle of the drive before lifting his hand in a final wave. It had been good to see him, even for a few fleeting minutes. Those old feelings she thought had been long buried bubbled to the surface. She waited until he was farther down the drive before she returned the wave. Not that he was looking in the rearview mirror. She was just the girl from his youth, and he must have a wonderful woman in Dallas. Nice guys like Hank always had someone special.

After she checked on Tony tinkering with the cider press, she crossed to the tractor and settled into the seat. Plowing didn't get done just thinking about it and with another few hours, she could make a huge dent in the task. After that she needed to do some research on semi-dwarf trees; was there anything different she'd need to do after staking them?

. . .

It had been a long day bouncing around in the seat on the old tractor. Renee walked out of the bathroom, wrapped in a cozy terrycloth robe, rubbing a hand towel over her hair. She sat down at her desk and reread the webpage she found regarding her new trees. Hank had not only bought new stock, but the variety that interested her most was the apple that was well suited for cider. She wanted to expand that part of the business and it was as if he remembered a long-ago, almost-forgotten conversation. She had shared so many of her dreams for the orchard while they watched the stars as they lay in the back of his truck bed on warm summer nights.

Hank had always wanted to be a lawyer and he fulfilled that dream. She wanted to be a farmer. It was as if they both got what they wanted. She glanced at a framed photo on her desk; it was the last photo of the two of them with friends from high school. It was right before everyone left for college that fall. They'd promised to not let the real world drive a wedge between them, but things happened and they broke it off. Maybe she should have packed away the photos her mom had left sitting out, but the memories were bittersweet and as time went by, it was more sweet than bitter.

Her cell rang. She didn't bother to look at the screen, assuming it was her mom as there wasn't anyone else she expected.

"Hello, Mom."

A deep, soft chuckle made her stomach flip. She remembered that laugh, letting it slip around her like a warm hug.

"It's Hank."

"Hello. This is unexpected."

"I was waiting for you to call and when you didn't, I wanted to make sure you got the delivery. I checked the tracking and it said the trees arrived."

She shook her head. She had promised to call and didn't. "I'm sorry, Hank. They did and the stock looks strong. Thank you for arranging everything. It was above and beyond."

"Good, I'm glad. Are you planting tomorrow?"

She pressed a hand to her lower back, stiff from driving the tractor, and tomorrow it would be even more achy. "That's the plan."

"It should be a good weather day and rest assured, the cattle won't be visiting again. The fence has been fixed."

She smiled into the phone. With a laugh, she said, "Good to know. Well, thanks for calling."

"Shout if you need anything. I'm only as far away as a few taps on your phone."

She didn't want to end the conversation. It was like the old days; Hank's quick wit about mundane details had a way of making her laugh in all situations.

"Thanks again for finding the new stock." She knew she was repeating herself but talking with him had thrown her off her game. "Even though these trees won't bear fruit for a couple of years, it's still…" Her voice trailed off. Would he understand a good day on the farm was like gold?

"Life in Montana isn't for the faint of heart and we have to make use of each good day before the cold and snow settles back in. So, I get it."

Ranch life wasn't much different than farm life in this part of the country but there wasn't any place she'd rather be even after Hank moved on again.

"Well, I've got a busy day ahead of me so have a good night, and Hank, you're a good friend."

"It takes one to know one, Renee. Sleep well."

She didn't get up from the chair immediately until a chill stole over her. With one last look at Hank's smiling face, she shut off the desk lamp.

4

The next morning Hank woke with Renee on his mind, and he couldn't shake the feeling she needed help but was too proud to ask. When he was at her farm yesterday, he heard someone working in one of the barns, but it seemed to be an operation for one. He got ready for the day and followed the smell of fresh-brewed coffee to the kitchen where his parents were enjoying a cup.

"Morning," he said to them both. As he poured a mug of steaming coffee, his stomach grumbled. Nothing like working hard during the day to wake up ravenous the next morning. "I'm going to get my work done early and then head over to the Mitchell place."

Mom pushed back from the table. "Let me get a plate for you."

He placed a hand on her shoulder. "No need to wait on me." He picked up a napkin-covered plate from the sideboard and discovered eggs and sausage links with a corn muffin for good measure. Now this would hit the spot and stick to his ribs. He dragged the chair across the old linoleum floor. "Anyone need a refill on coffee before I sit?"

"No, thanks." Dad leveled a look at him. "What are you going to do at the Mitchell farm?"

He added hot sauce to his eggs and buttered his muffin and as an afterthought added a dollop of his mom's home-made apple butter.

"When I stopped over yesterday, it was like a ghost town over there. I could see someone had the tractor out; it had fresh clumps of dirt on the plow blade. Except for hearing someone working in a barn, I didn't see another soul. I get the impression she's going to try and plant the trees by herself and that's a lot more than any one person can handle."

Mom gave him a gentle smile. "You always did have a tender spot for Renee, all the way back to grade school."

She wasn't wrong but now was not the time to admit it. "It's the neighborly thing to do, so I'll check in with Louie before I head out and make sure he's all set, but I can't stand the thought of her working hard by herself when I can lend some muscle."

"You're probably right."

Dad was nodding which made this conversation a little easier.

"Do you think you should take a couple men with you?"

That was a very generous offer from Dad. "Let me scope out the situation and if I'm right, we might just need to do that. I ordered close to six hundred trees."

"Isn't that too many?" he asked.

"When I talked to the customer service person at the wholesale nursery, they said you can actually put anywhere from one to three hundred per acre so I split the difference."

Dad's brow shot up. "Did our cattle damage that many trees?"

"Not exactly, but I couldn't get full size so I bought enough to plant the field they were in." He shoveled the eggs into his mouth. This conversation was beginning to probe a little too deep and there were unasked questions he didn't want to face.

He steered the conversation to driving the cattle to higher ground for grazing and swayed from the topic of a certain pretty redhead with velvety-brown eyes. After putting his dishes in the dishwasher, he kissed the top of Mom's head and said he'd check in before he took off.

*H*ank pulled up in front of one of the brick-red barns that bore the Riverbend Orchard logo. It was a bit weathered but still stood out to welcome people who came to pick apples each fall. He glanced around as he strode to the house. All he could hear was birds chirping, and the parking lot was devoid of vehicles in what he guessed was the employee lot, so his hunch was starting to look correct. In addition, there were pallets of root stock placed around the area too.

He rapped on the glass pane in the kitchen door. The late morning sun was rising higher in the cloudless blue sky. He hadn't expected anyone to answer but logically it was the best place to start.

He got back in his truck and headed out to where he guessed he'd find Renee. He glanced at the cooler on the passenger seat; he'd stopped to pack water and sandwiches, enough for both of them, along with the cookies Mom had insisted he take.

The truck bounced along the rutted lane, highlighting the need for fresh gravel, at least in the deepest holes. It was a wonder she didn't break a tractor axel, but then again, she probably knew right where they were and drove around them. Well, he'd know for next time.

He rested his arm in the open window, enjoying the simple pleasure before thinking of when he'd be headed back to Dallas as soon as Dad was up and mobile. There might not be another time he'd drive down this lane.

When he took a left turn, he saw the tractor in the distance hauling a flatbed trailer loaded to the edges with trees. He scanned the area. Just as he thought, there wasn't another person in sight. He gripped the steering wheel and tamped down the annoyance. Why hadn't she asked for help? Stubborn pride. That was the reason he'd work right alongside her and get it done, and for his pay, he was taking her out for pie. Maybe not tonight but soon.

He parked the truck under a large apple tree, its canopy filled with blossoms. If nothing else, it looked like this year's harvest was promising. He waited as the tractor began to head back in his direction. She slowed and came to a stop.

Sitting in the seat of the tractor, she gave him a tight smile. "Hank, what are you doing here? Don't you have something that needs your attention over at Stone's Throw? Like fixing fences or something?"

He shrugged and made sure a wide grin was plastered on his face, one he hoped was irresistible. "As a matter of fact, I'm free and thought I might keep you company, being old friends and all."

She gave him the stink eye, the one where she crossed her arms over her midsection and tilted her head down, eyes narrowed. It nearly took his breath away. He hadn't realized until that moment how much he missed this woman.

"If I had wanted your help, I would have asked when we talked last night."

He took a few steps in her direction. "Are you saying you have so much help you can't use an extra pair of hands?"

That was one way to challenge her without stating the obvious.

"I have people."

Thankfully the fencing had arrived, but she had to buy new tree stock and pay people to plant, and she had already done that once. If things were as tight as he thought, she'd try to go it alone.

"I'm sure you do but I've got a few guys who aren't busy so I'd like to bring them over and pitch in. You can oversee us all."

He watched her shoulders droop and he could only guess the burden she was carrying.

"Look, I get it. You've taken over the farm and it's a hard and fickle business. Accepting some help for something you had zero control over doesn't mean you're any less capable. But it shows your willingness to put your personal feelings aside for the sake of your business."

"I don't know…" She looked across the newly plowed field.

"Renee, if I was in a tight spot, would you help me?"

She gave him an appraising look as if she was measuring her words carefully. After a few moments, she said, "Probably."

He rubbed his hands together and grinned. "Good.

Give me a couple of minutes to call the ranch and we can get started."

She waited while he made a quick call to Dad; reinforcements would be over within the hour. Depending on how many guys were free, it might be possible to get all the trees in the ground today. Having a mechanical planter was something she wouldn't have since most orchards didn't replant trees every year.

He withdrew two bottles of water and a bag of cookies from the cooler. He wasn't above using his mom's cookies as a way to sweeten her up, and he happened to know she was partial to any cookie his mom made.

She was still sitting on the tractor when he sauntered back over to her. He tossed a bottle that she caught with ease, and then he dangled the baggie. "Cookie?"

Her eyes brightened. "Your mom's?"

"Of course." He stepped up onto the narrow tractor step and perched on the fender. "Where do you want to start?" He looked over his shoulder at the neatly stacked pallets on the wagon. "Did you load all of these today?"

With a lighthearted chuckle, she said, "I'm not Wonder Woman." She snagged a cookie from the bag and Hank couldn't help himself; he took two.

She rolled her eyes while she groaned with pleasure as she took a bite of the cookie. Once upon a time she used to —well, he wasn't going to dwell on the pleasure he took when he kissed her.

With a grin, she said, "I had the truck driver unload directly onto the wagon; it saved me a lot of work this morning."

"Always thinking, just like when we were younger."

"Speaking of." She flipped the key and the engine sputtered to a low grumble. "Let's unload out in the furthest spot and go back to the barn and load up again."

"If we time it right, the guys might be here to help." He unsnapped his shirt pocket and pulled out his cell phone. "I'll let them know to meet us at the barn."

She held up her hands, palm side up. "Whatever." She placed her lips on his cheek, in a featherlight kiss. "I'm done protesting so thank you."

His heart skipped a beat with the brush of her lips. If he turned his head, he'd love to see if he could make her sigh too. But he reminded himself to keep this friendly and not overcomplicate things between them or worse, start something he couldn't finish.

He held up a finger. "Dad, can you let the guys know to meet us at the barn? We'll need to load up the trailer and get the trees out to the field."

He listened. "Sure thing, and Joe had them bring over a couple of trailers too, thinking you'd get all the stock out to the field in one shot."

Efficiency was his dad's middle name and it didn't surprise Hank he had put everything in motion. He was about to hang up when Dad said, "Hold on a minute; Mom wants to talk to you."

"Hank, it's Mom."

He grinned. It was so like his mother to make an announcement for something he already knew but she was the sweetest woman so what did it matter? "Hey, Mom."

"Would you ask Renee if she'd like to come for dinner tonight? I won't take no for an answer. After working all day, she'll probably eat a bowl of cereal and she needs a decent meal."

"I'll ask her but I'm not guaranteeing anything."

She cocked a brow and mouthed, What?

"Just remind her that I've driven over to pick her up before when she turned me down so tonight could be a repeat performance."

"Yes, ma'am. I'll tell her." He stuck the phone in his shirt pocket. "Mom said you need to come for dinner and if you refuse, she's coming to pick you up."

"Like she did when my parents went on vacation when I was in college and I stayed home. Your mom got it into her head I was gonna wither away and starve before they returned and it was only for a long weekend." She smiled as they slipped down memory lane. "Dinner sounds good."

At a loss by her quick agreement, he said, "We should unload; otherwise, Mom will be looking for us."

She dropped the tractor in gear and he observed her from the corner of his eye. She was even more beautiful, if it was possible, and he felt that old tug inside. He could keep denying he had romantic feelings for her, but he was lying to himself. Time hadn't changed his heart.

5

Renee grabbed the iron rake and smoothed out the dirt around the base on the last tree in this section. They were more than half done and it was going better than she'd hoped. The ranch hands worked harder than anyone she had hired. Maybe it was because there wasn't anything extra in this from her, but then it dawned on her. The people she hired were on the clock; if they took their time, they got paid more.

She kicked a clod of dirt toward the next tree and Hank looked over at her.

"What's on your mind?"

She straightened the roots on the next tree. "Nothing." She did her best to mask her annoyance and turned away from him. No sense seeing if he could still figure out what she was thinking at almost any given moment. It had always been that way between the two of them; with one look and a question, there would be no secrets between them and she needed to keep a few—mainly the big one. Old feelings had busted through the crusty shell over her heart and she had come to realize she'd never stopped loving him. It wasn't immature love; it had been the real thing.

She glanced at his guys and back to the hole she was setting a tree into.

"So, it's like that?" His voice was as smooth as honey.

She lifted her eyes to meet his. "What are you talking about?"

"Either you're unhappy with the job we're doing or you're unhappy with the previous crew."

She clenched her hands around the shovel and proceeded to widen the hole. "Just stop doing that."

"Working?"

She pointed her index finger at him. "In addition to planting trees, your brain is pitching like a bucking stallion with a burr under his saddle."

"I can't help it if I'm concerned." He lifted a shoulder and dropped it.

She could barely hear what he said next. "Hank, if you have something to say, speak up." He was just poking at her so she'd fess up, but it wasn't going to work. Not this time.

"I said it's too bad you didn't have decent help not just to get the trees planted but the fence up too."

She didn't need to be reminded about the stupid fence. It had been a calculated risk but it was the first time a bunch of dumb cows wandered across the river. How was she supposed to know they had a section of fence down?

"There are only so many hours in a day." The shovel bit into the softened earth and she silently thanked her lucky stars for that; the planting was going smoothly.

He began to unload more trees and paused, leaning against the back of the wagon. "I'll make a deal with you."

Past experience reminded her Hank never made a deal

he didn't intend on winning. But curiosity would get the best of her in the long run so it was better just to ask now and save them both some time. "I'll bite."

He pushed the brim of his cowboy hat back with his finger, like a gunslinger in an old spaghetti western. A glint lit up his eyes. If it were one hundred years in the past, she'd guess his fingers would be flexing, getting ready to draw if the deal wasn't agreed to, but he wasn't wearing a six-gun on his hip and Hank would never hurt any living creature.

"If my men get the trees planted today, we'll come back tomorrow and get that fence of yours installed."

"What's in it for you?" She cocked her head and narrowed her eyes. What could he possibly have up his sleeve?

"If we pull through with both of these jobs, not only will you have dinner at my parents tonight, but tomorrow night we'll go out for dinner and pie at the Filler Up."

Somehow it sounded almost too good to be true. Not only would her trees get planted, but she'd have a fence and two good dinners she didn't have to cook.

"Sounds like you'll be getting the short end of the straw." But it would give her an excellent excuse to see him a couple more times before he went back to Dallas. The downside was she was going to miss him even more. But what the heck, it was better to have loved and lost than never to have loved at all, right?

She thrust out her hand and gave his a firm shake. Before she released it, she squeezed. "Just so we're clear, your guys have to finish today and get the fence up tomor-row, right?"

"That's right."

She was almost a little disappointed. There was no way

they'd get all the fencing done in one day, not with the six of them working from dawn till dusk, and the ranch hands had other responsibilities too.

A grin blossomed across his face and he held her hand a little longer than necessary. "Just remember, you put zero conditions on this deal."

Her radar pinged like a bat at night. Hank was up to something and by the smirk on his face, she thought she'd just made a deal with a handsome devil. "Trees and fencing. Not much else to say."

He let out an ear-piercing whistle and his guys looked up. He waved his arm overhead like he was using a lasso on an errant cow. But in this instance, it was telling them to speed things up. He got a thumbs-up from one of the men. Then he withdrew his cell and punched in a few numbers.

"Dad, we need some more men over here. We've got fencing to install and we'll need all the equipment to go with it." He listened and grinned. "And can you tell Mom to make up her famous chocolate cake for dessert? Yeah, Renee's favorite." He gave her a saucy wink and her heart skipped a couple of beats. She knew she'd walked right into that deal with her eyes wide open.

Not that it mattered. She was going to enjoy the next couple of days and extract every bit of fun she could.

He returned his cell to his jeans pocket. "And that's how a deal is won."

"All right, smart aleck, you may have set things in motion, but the trees aren't in yet and there's a lot of fencing to be installed."

"Darlin', if there's one thing you should never forget when it comes to me, I always finish what I start, and all that's left to determine is what time I'm picking you up tomorrow night."

She did love his confidence and he was right about one thing. Hank Shepard always found a way to make whatever he wanted happen and on his schedule too.

"Seven o'clock would be just fine."

He waved a hand in front of her. "Six. We want to make sure we have plenty of time to linger over dinner and dessert and if you play your cards right, I might just take you out for a little stargazing too."

"Cocky." She grinned and walked away but not before she said over her shoulder, "Stargazing is on the table if you play your cards right."

He laughed loud and long as she continued to plant trees; after all, two dates were riding on getting this job done on time.

*H*ank had picked her up at exactly six and dinner had been such fun. From the corner of her eye, she looked at his profile. His parents, Henry and Maeve, were gracious as always, and on her lap were two large slices of the chocolate cake Maeve had insisted she take with her. It'd be delicious with her morning coffee, but after she ate something like eggs to counterbalance all the sugar and butter.

"Thanks for tonight. I had a good time and I'm glad your mom insisted that I come."

"They loved seeing you. I didn't realize you hadn't been over for dinner since you've been back."

They bumped along a well-worn dirt road on their way to the overlook, a place where they had spent lots of evenings when they were in high school. The spot had been her idea and Hank was quick to agree; it held a lot of special memories for them. It was the place where they had their first kiss, first fight, and first make-up kissing session too. It was also the place where they made the decision to go their separate ways for college, of course with the promise they'd never lose track of the other.

She looked out the window and thought how naïve they had been. "Do you ever think about that night?"

In this case she was glad explanations weren't necessary. He'd know what she referred to.

"All the time." He gave her hand a squeeze and she absorbed his warmth like she'd been brought in from a Montana winter and set in front of a roaring fire.

"Do you have regrets?" His voice was soft, and the tenor of his voice matched the beat of her heart, slow and steady.

"Regrets aren't how I live my life. I always look forward but I like to learn from the past."

He slowed as they approached the old ponderosa pine grove. Once he parked, he released his seat belt and turned toward her. "There are times where I wish we had a do-over. If I could go back to the younger me, I'd tell myself to find a way to keep in touch, do the work to stay friends."

"But we had to follow our dreams." That was how she had thought about the past too. If only.

"We did, but our friendship would have kept us connected and I've missed your honesty and way of looking at life. You never let me skate by when things got tough; you challenged me to reach for the stars."

"Did you touch any?" She swallowed the lump in her throat. Being with him, here, tonight was harder than she thought it would be.

"I did but it was a hollow victory without you telling me to stretch beyond, to keep pushing and find new goals." The sound of his voice was thick with emotion and words he wanted to say but held back. Being with Hank tonight was as if no time had passed between them, and she knew by the way he looked at her and touched her hand he felt it too.

"And now?" Did she dare hope that he would say something to lead them down the road to a new future?

"I'm confused. I came back to help out Dad and I never expected to run into you much less spend time with you."

She withdrew her hand. She could hear an end coming in his words and it would be easier to handle if she wasn't touching him.

"The more time we spend together the more confused I get." His finger traced along her jawline and he tipped her chin up before lowering his lips to hers. It was a gentle and tender kiss with raw emotion bubbling under the surface.

She wanted to reach out and keep kissing him but that wasn't the right thing to do. He was leaving; Dallas was his home now just as her home was Montana. She had to keep reminding herself of this hard truth.

"I think you should take me home now."

6

———————

ank was stunned. The last thing he had expected was for Renee to ask him to take her home. He wanted to stay out here all night like they used to do, talking about their hopes and dreams for the future, just being together. But the words she just said threw ice water over him.

He drove them back to the farm; the ride was quiet and Renee had withdrawn into herself. But they had tomorrow working on the fence together, and then she had promised him dinner out. Would it be right to hold her to the promise? Even if he wanted to, he'd never pressure her into going; it was all in her hands. He glanced her way and the sad expression on her face tore at his insides. What had he done to cause her so much pain? He replayed what he had said and done but nothing came to mind. They had been enjoying their time together and once they started talking about reaching for the stars, he should have said it was hollow without her by his side. But he couldn't admit that to her; she'd think less of him, wouldn't she?

He pulled up next to the side porch of the farmhouse

and turned off the truck. Before she could get out, he said, "Please wait a moment."

He hurried around to the passenger side and opened the door for her, holding out his hand. Her fingers grazed his and sent his heart into a stampede. He walked her to the door and stood under the same porch light he had stood under a thousand times before.

"Renee, I don't know what I said that made you sad, but I'm sorry. I wanted tonight to be enjoyable for both of us."

"You didn't do anything; it's just the way our lives turned out. We're on different paths. Soon you'll be headed back to Dallas and I'll be growing apples. We're both where we want to be, and it wouldn't do any good to pretend otherwise. Thank you for taking me to your parents' place and for the drive." She stood on tiptoes and brushed her lips over his cheek.

The smell of her soft floral scent teased his senses. It was another sucker punch to the gut, a reminder of what once was.

She stepped back and opened the door. She looked at him as if memorizing his face. "I'll understand if you don't want to come around tomorrow to help with the fence. I'll take care of it."

He tipped his head. "And if I want to?"

Her face softened into a small smile. "I've learned to never refuse an act of genuine kindness."

"What about the second half of our bargain?" His heart thumped in his chest and his mouth went dry. He hoped she'd say they were still on for dinner tomorrow night.

She looked up through her lashes. "The fence isn't finished yet so no telling if we'll be going out tomorrow night."

His heart soared; she wasn't saying no. "No worries, that fence will be up and secured before dinnertime."

Her laugh caressed his ears. It was something he could hear for the rest of his life. Before he could think about anything else, she wished him a good night and softly closed the door, leaving him standing under the porch light alone.

He walked back to his truck and with a glance at the house, he could see her progress as she flicked on lights in each room. She had never been a fan of the dark and in a small way it was nice to see that some things hadn't changed.

Tomorrow when they had dinner, he'd see if he could keep that sweet smile on her face. He dropped the truck in gear. Before he went home, he'd swing by the bunkhouse to make sure all hands were ready to get the fence done. He'd even reached out to his old friend, Lincoln Cooper, at the Grace Star Ranch for extra hands to get the job finished. He knew how to make things happen and he wasn't about to take any chances on blowing his date with Renee.

The next morning was overcast as Hank hopped in his truck for the short ride over to Renee's place. She was going to be surprised when she saw all the people who had come to pitch in. On his way down the drive, he noticed a bunch of guys loading pickup trucks with tools, and there was post hole digger attached to a tractor. Linc said he'd bring one over too so all that was left to do was get started.

His tires kicked up dust as he drove down Renee's driveway and he swung by her house but guessed she was already out in the orchard since her tractor was gone but he'd double-check. He wondered why she didn't have an auger attached to her tractor but maybe being a farm, it was more cost-effective to rent one from the Trading Post Hardware in town. After his knock went unanswered, he headed out to the fields. He slowed as he approached the first area they had planted and there she was, unhooking a flatbed wagon that was filled with posts. His admiration for her grew. She might be getting help today, but she wasn't one to sit by and let people do all the work for her.

"Renee." He waved his arms, hoping to get her attention. He didn't want to walk up on her and potentially scare her. She had a hair-trigger sense of flight or fight and the woman was holding some kind of tool in her hands. "Renee," he shouted again as he got closer. She was really concentrating on what she was working on.

She looked up and shielded her eyes with the back of her hand. "Hank, what are you doing here already?"

He held up his arm where his watch normally rested. "As a rancher, former or present, we get up early to start our day. The cattle don't sleep in."

She tossed a set of cutters on the edge of the wagon. "I didn't expect you so early. I thought I'd get a jump on things." She looked over his shoulder. "Are you by yourself?"

"A couple of guys will be along soon. They were loading up when I left."

A grin twitched her lips. "Looks like no dinner for us tonight."

He jammed his hands in his jeans pockets. "Is that hope or disappointment in your voice?"

"Well, you just said"—she did air quotes—"a couple of guys are headed this way, but you and I both know it's gonna take a small but mighty army of people to get this fence up and around the acreage."

"We're talking around four thousand feet of fence. Not to worry, we'll be done by sundown."

She made a *tsk tsk* sound and shook her head. "You're awfully confident, Shepard. Care to make the bet double or nothing?"

He gave her a side-eye look. "Huh, how about we agree that if the fence is finished, not only will you have dinner in town with me tonight, but we'll take a picnic down to the river over the weekend."

"Do I have to pack said picnic basket?" She was trying to keep the grin from growing.

"Nope."

She tapped her chin. "But at the moment this little bargain only gives you what you want. How about if you don't succeed? What do I get?"

"I think our arrangement suits us both but go ahead if you want to sweeten your side of the agreement. Tell me what you'd like." He leaned up against the side of the wagon, wishing she'd spill it. All too soon the jig would be up, and she'd know that the army she thought didn't exist would be pulling in soon.

"I can't think of anything under all this pressure, so if the fence isn't finished, you'll agree I can tweak the bargain and you'll have to agree." She stuck out her hand. "What do you say?"

He could see the sparkle in her eyes and this was a no-brainer. He'd always do whatever she wanted but by the end of today, her new trees would be protected and he'd have two dates with this lovely woman standing in front of him. He clasped her hand with his and then covered the top of her hand with his other one.

"I can't wait to see your face when we drive the last fence post and secure the last section." He gave her a wink. "And if I might suggest wearing something blue tonight, it makes your eyes pop."

A low rumble from the road drew her attention. The army had arrived. Her eyes widened. "Hank, how many favors did you have to call in?"

Two tractors with augers and pickup trucks with flatbed trailers were right behind them.

"No favors. I just asked good friends to lend a hand." He brushed back a lock of hair from her cheek. "They're your friends too, Renee."

Her mouth hung open and she was speechless for several long moments. She brushed away the tears that appeared on her lashes and murmured, "Thank you."

He pulled his leather gloves from his back pocket. He hadn't wanted to make her cry, even if they were tears of joy. "Come on, sunshine. It's fencing time."

*H*ank's mom showed up with his dad riding shotgun in her SUV. She had baskets of food for lunch, more than enough for everyone. She knew what fencing day was like having lived through many in her years on the ranch. Dad waved from the vehicle and Hank walked over to him.

"Hey, Dad, how's it looking?"

"Real good. Do I see Linc Cooper over there?"

"You do and he brought nine of his men so all together we're running a crew of twenty-two including me and Renee."

"Good thing your mom packed the entire kitchen to

feed everyone." He gave Hank a wide smile. "A nice thing you're doing here."

"I'd do anything for her." He turned and watched as she pulled a roll of metal fence wire from the back of the wagon. She had shown everyone right from the start of the day she'd hold her own.

"Except move back to Montana?"

Hank was taken aback by the question. "Why, do you think she would welcome me back?"

"I saw the way she looked at you last night and some things haven't changed at all. There's not many times in life you get a second chance with the woman you've always loved, and in case you haven't noticed, she's unattached and so are you."

"I have a law practice in Texas."

"I happen to know you passed the bar in two states so the only thing that is preventing you from moving home, is you."

Mom made her way over to the SUV. "What are you two talking about?"

Hank glanced at his father. "Mending fences."

"And building them," Dad said.

He knew exactly what his father wanted to hear and now was not the time to discuss his love life, least of all with his parents. He dropped a kiss on the top of his mom's head.

"Thanks for bringing lunch over. I won't be home for dinner."

"A date with someone we know?" Mom's eyes twinkled and there was a hopeful note in her voice. She had never made it a secret that Renee and Hank should get back together and had always said they were like two peas in a pod.

"Dinner with a very good friend." He opened the driver's door for her. "Thanks again and I'll bring home the baskets." She got in and he leaned down. "Watch out for the potholes on your way out."

Dad gave him a wink. "You've got time for another project before you leave. I'm stepping back into the day-to-day workings of our ranch; my sick leave is over."

"Dad, did you just fire me?" He wanted to laugh but his father had an ulterior motive that was clear as a pane of glass.

"Someone needs to take action and if you're not willing, I can."

Hank watched as his parents left. The road was something he could fix.

$\mathcal{R}$enee rifled through her closet in search of a blue top to go with her new slim-fitting black Wranglers. She should be exhausted but after the day she put in working side by side with Hank, she was exhilarated. The fence was finished and she could stop worrying about the new trees. In a few years, there would be fruit. She walked to the window and looked out over the orchard. She had the best view from any room in the house over what was now her business.

At times she had been lonely as a child, but if she had siblings, she wouldn't have free rein over the future of Riverbend. Well, other than Dad giving her the occasional unsolicited advice. She smiled when she thought how he'd be proud of all that had been accomplished over the last few days and it had gone from rotten apples to sweet cider.

Her analogies were always lame which is why she never told anyone how her brain worked—well, except for Hank. He always knew and when they were younger, he thought she was quirky in a sweet way.

She turned back to the closet and pulled out a deep-blue print blouse. That would work with jeans and she'd wear the alligator boots she bought before she left the city. She added a touch of plum lipstick and she was ready for the night. Hopefully she wasn't overdressed for the diner, even if it was the best diner she'd ever eaten in. Maggie Brady had taken it over from her parents which was common around town; businesses often became generational.

A toot caught her attention and she pulled back the sheer curtain. Hank was right on time. She felt like she wanted to skip down the stairwell, but this wasn't a date date. Just dinner with her good friend who happened to make her knees wobble like jelly when he gave her that crooked grin.

She heard him cross the porch to the back door. Before he could knock, she took a deep calming breath and pulled it open.

Her eyes dropped to the bunch of bright-yellow flowers with a light-brown center. He remembered she loved arrowleaf balsamroot, an early flower that grew around here but not on her land. He must have found a patch on the way over.

"For you."

"Thank you." She took them and went into the kitchen; they needed to be put in water. She grabbed a glass pitcher she normally made tea in, but it would be the perfect substitute for a vase. It really was sweet of him, and she looked at him from under her lashes. Did he remember or was it just a lucky guess?

"Are they still your favorites?" Tall with wide shoulders, he filled the doorway. Her heart skipped again. She needed to get her feelings under control before she had an angina attack. She smiled at the thought. He had already zapped her heart; it was hammering in her chest right now and it was good to feel the blood pulsing in her veins. "Yes, they're still my favorites. It was sweet you remembered."

"There's very little I forget and that includes simple pleasures like flowers and"—he pulled a chocolate bar from his shirt pocket and handed it to her—"dark chocolate with coconut."

If things were different she would have thrown her arms around his neck and kissed him senseless. The gesture was thoughtful and he was right; the simple things did mean the most.

She crooked her finger and he came closer. Throwing caution to the wind, she brushed her lips over his. She drank in his woodsy cologne and on his breath, she could smell the lingering aroma of the same sweet treat he had just given her. She swatted his arm as she stepped back. "You had one?"

He laughed and slipped his arms around her waist, pulling her close to his chest. "Quality control purposes only." He lowered his mouth to hers but stopped when there was a wisp of air between them. Waiting for her to make the next move.

She tipped her head to the side and gave him a slow, sweet kiss. But as her thoughts began to cloud her better judgment, she stepped back and looked at the floor. She didn't want him to see the love she knew would be in her eyes. In the last three days she had not only cracked the protective shell over her heart but tossed it on the garbage pile. But she wasn't about to throw caution to the wind.

"I don't know about you, but I've worked up quite the appetite. I wonder what Maggie's got for specials tonight."

He took half a step back as if he understood her withdrawal and respected it. "Don't forget to save room for pie too."

"I might even bring a slice home." She slung her bag across her body and took the house keys from the table. "I'm ready."

He pushed open the door and let her walk out ahead of him. The sun wasn't ready to call it a day for another hour. She loved it as the days grew longer; even in late April the sun went down after eight.

At the end of the driveway Hank turned onto the main road which led into town.

Renee looked over at his handsome profile, his strong jawline and mouth always quick with a smile. "Have you been to the diner since you've been back?"

"No, I was busy with the ranch and for a while Dad was in the hospital and then rehab. When he came home, Mom was making all his favorite meals, which happen to be mine too so there wasn't a need to go into town."

"Getting your fill of home cooking is never a bad idea, especially when your mom's in front of the stove."

"She's pretty talented but so is your mom; her brownies are amazing. Will your parents come back this summer?"

"That's the plan. I think sometime in late June maybe." It would break up the quiet and she could pick Dad's brain about the cider press too. If she was going to grow the business, a better understanding of why he made the decisions he had could prove to be invaluable.

"I'll be sorry I missed them."

And there it was, a sharp reminder their time together was fleeting. But that wasn't something she needed to think about for tonight. "I'll give them your best." Her throat was tight as they turned down Main Street, past the bank, movie theater, and hardware store before he pulled up in front of the diner. From outside she could see it was bustling with midweek activity which meant tables would be at a premium and they might need to wait.

They walked inside and Maggie's smile welcomed them. "Hey, you two. I wondered when you'd find your way in for dinner." She pointed to a booth near the back. "Take a seat and I'll be right over."

Renee looked around. Not much had changed with black-and-white floor tiles, booths along the front windows with their bright-blue vinyl cushions, tables packed in close, and the counter with short stools near the kitchen with a mirror over the pass-through so people at the counter could watch what was going on behind them and watch Mack, who was older than dirt, put out mouth-watering meals every day. He'd been here for as long as Renee could remember and there was nobody that could make mouthwatering pancakes like him.

Hank let her choose which bench seat she wanted but for a change she didn't want to look at the comings and goings of people; she wanted to focus on Hank.

He gave a hoot of laughter. "Look at this. The menu is still printed on the paper placemats."

"The best things never change, Hank." She wanted to say, look at me and how I feel about you, that didn't change even though I tried to push my feelings aside. Instead, she pretended to study the menu.

Maggie came over and rattled off the dinner specials and then left them to decide.

"Do you want to share two different meals?"

He looked up and grinned. "What are you thinking?"

"The chicken fried steak and fried chicken with

dumplings. We're celebrating the completion of two major projects." She tapped the placemat at the drink list. "But I'll skip the shake in favor of pie after. My metabolism isn't what it was when we were teenagers."

"Truth. I'll have to hit the gym regularly when I'm back home. I've gotten used to eating more."

A knife twisted in her gut as he referred to Dallas as his home. "You don't need a gym out here."

He passed her a paper napkin. "I've forgotten all the different muscles you use when working out here. I'll admit I had a few days of sore muscles. But it's all good now."

After they gave Maggie their order, an uncomfortable silence settled over them. Hank fiddled with his fork and the napkin, stabbing little holes into the paper.

"Tell me about Chicago. Did you like living there?"

That seemed like a lifetime ago now. She'd been home almost four months and not once did she think about going back to the insanity of traffic and the congestion of people. It was something she hadn't recognized until her inner spring had unwound once she started working and living at the orchard.

"I was happy there and I enjoyed my job designing office spaces for corporations. They wanted to make them feel less sterile and more comfortable since so many people spend a lot of time at the office. I wanted people to feel good like it was a home away from home if that makes any sense."

"And did you find someone special?"

No sense in skirting the truth. "I dated but never found that special connection with any guy I met." And it was definitely not like how she felt being with Hank now.

"What about you? Does big city life trip your trigger?"

Her heart thudded. She knew it did or why would he keep talking about going back like it didn't matter.

"I like my job at the law firm; it keeps me on my toes and there isn't much time for fun."

"There's no one waiting for you back home?" She held her breath, waiting for him to say the words she didn't want to hear.

"Nope. Like you, I've never made that special connection with anyone besides you."

Was he acknowledging the connection they still shared? She looked at him, barely breathing.

"What, you're not involved?"

He reached across the bright-white Formica table and waited for her to take his hand. She placed her hand in his and his warmth spread through her.

"Renee, you're impossible to forget." He gave her hand a squeeze. "And I'm hoping I might be unforgettable too."

That was almost her undoing. He knew her favorite song was by Nat King Cole and now he linked that to this conversation. Should she be bold and speak the undeniable truth or would putting her heart on the line make her a fool? Heck, she was taking chances in every aspect of her life, leaving a lucrative career to be a farmer, and that was a career path that wasn't for the faint of heart.

"I still love you, but I'm not expecting anything from you."

8

———————

*S*tunned didn't begin to describe how he felt the moment Renee said she was still in love with him. But in the next breath, she seemed to dismiss those feelings too.

He wished there wasn't a table between them or that they weren't in a public building. He'd take her in his arms and show her just how much he loved her. Her face drooped and she tore at the paper napkin in her hands. Was sharing her innermost feelings unbearable for her?

Taking the napkin from her, Hank set it aside and dipped his head so that he could make eye contact. "That was the sweetest thing you've ever said to me."

She looked at him and a small smile graced her kissable lips. "I wanted to tell you how I feel, no matter what may come of our time together."

So that was it, the reason she had pulled back. The end of this moment in time. She recognized it but could they do something long distance? Although the miles between here and Dallas seemed endless, he'd make a point of coming home more often. He certainly had enough paid time off banked, and they could video chat and text. It was possible if they really wanted to stay connected.

He reached across the table and caressed her cheek. "We live in the twenty-first century and there's amazing technology so we can stay in touch—text, email, video calls, and airplanes."

"This isn't something we need to talk about tonight, Hank. We should enjoy our dinner and make plans for the picnic we're going on this weekend. Those are things we should be focused on, not trying to figure out how to keep in touch when you leave." She sat back against the vinyl cushion and tucked her hands in her lap.

He understood it was easier when they weren't touching, but he wanted to be close with her, and every time they seemed to take a step in that direction one of them pulled back.

Maggie came by and delivered their dinners along with two extra plates for sharing. "Enjoy." She bustled away to the next table, leaving them alone in a busy diner.

After they each passed half of their meals to the other, Hank sliced off a piece of chicken fried steak. As he savored the unique flavor, he thought about how they seemed to be tap-dancing around the topic of the past.

"Renee." He put his fork down. "I think we need to clear the air about what happened all those years ago."

Her eyes grew wide and she shook her head. "There's nothing to rehash. We were young and had strong feelings for each other, but as kids we didn't know how to make a long-distance relationship work."

He nodded in agreement but there was more to it than that. He was hurt she didn't pick up and follow him.

"And we had different goals in life. If I had just trotted along behind you, going to the college you attended just so we could be together, what did that say about me? I needed to find my own way in the world. Being an interior designer was important to me just as going into law was your dream. Like Robert Frost said, there were two roads in the wood; I happened to take the road that was best suited for me and you took the other."

"It would have been nice to go to college together."

She stopped cutting the steak and gave him a long look. He knew what that meant; she was measuring her words carefully.

"If I had asked you to go to college in Chicago instead of New York, would you have followed me?"

He blinked hard, completely taken off guard. They hadn't ever talked about him not attending NYU. It was his dream school.

"No, but there were great design schools in New York. It would have been easy, with your talent, to be accepted into any one of them."

She leaned forward. "That is exactly my point. You never even considered changing your plans. You always assumed I should change the direction of my life to suit you. I had an excellent opportunity with a full scholarship; why would I have turned that down just to be by your side?"

The challenge was in her voice and for the first time he heard how arrogant he sounded, like she needed to follow him just so that they could continue their romance. He had been a class A jerk only seeing his side this entire time.

"I can't believe I expected you to change your dream. I'm so sorry." And he meant it from the bottom of his heart, but he couldn't change what he had done in his youth. All he could do was show her he was a better man today, one who didn't have the expectation she'd pack up and follow him. Even the fleeting thought he'd had about her leaving the farm and moving to Dallas to work as a designer again was something that had been a remote possibility in his mind. He audibly groaned.

"Are you alright?" Genuine concern filled her soft-brown eyes. "Do you want to leave?" She held up her hand to get Maggie's attention.

He reached out and took it. "I'm fine other than I've just discovered I'm a stupid guy, so full of himself that I'm ashamed to even admit it out loud to you."

She laughed softly. "It's okay. I already knew you were a regular guy when it comes to some things, others you're kinda special."

He perked up. She did still think he had some good qualities. Now he had to know what they might be so he could build on them. "Do tell?"

She shook her head from side to side with a huge grin. "Nope, you'll need to figure that out all on your own."

And just like that they settled back into their comfortable banter but with a new awareness on his part that he needed to really think about what he expected from Renee, and maybe not just her but other people in his life, like his parents and co-workers. It was time to stop taking people for granted.

*T*he remainder of their dinner conversation was easy and they talked about their favorite movies and books they'd read. Despite the almost twenty-year separation, he was happy to hear some of her favorite adventure movies were his too. He went to pay the check and she pulled it from his hand.

"After all the work you've put in on my farm the last

two days, the least I can do is buy dinner." She nodded in the direction of two brown paper boxes on the table. "And dessert."

The spark in her eye told him she wasn't taking no for an answer so rather than debate it, he'd let it go. But the picnic was on him, and he planned on going all out with all her favorite foods and beverages. One of the ways he could show her how much he cared was creating a very special memory.

He draped his arm around her shoulders, and she slipped hers around his waist as they walked down the main street. She tipped her head back. "Just look at those stars." Their steps slowed. "Look, there's the Big Dipper."

She had always been good at finding the constellations. "Do you still have that telescope you got for Christmas one year?"

"I do, but it's kind of late to set that up."

He wondered if she was tired. It had been a very busy few days and besides the physical labor, there had been a bit of an emotional journey for them both.

"How about we take it with us this Sunday and we can stargaze."

"I was thinking, how about we go on Saturday instead. On Sunday I wanted to sleep in. Not that I'm an old lady or anything, but six days a week I'm super busy and if we want to watch the stars, it'll be a late night, which will make for a long week."

That made sense. Since coming home, he'd made it a point to have Sundays off too to ease into the day, check work email, and basically use it as an office day.

"Sounds like a great idea. Do you think we can head out to the river by six? I'll be done with chores if you can wrap up your day too."

She held him a little closer to her body and said, "Six it is. What should I pack?"

"Not a thing. I've got it covered."

"But..."

He dropped a kiss on her cheek. "The deal was you'd have to go on a picnic with me, not that you had to fill the basket too."

She smothered a yawn. "That's not how I understood it."

She was tired so they turned back toward his truck. "My motivation for the deal was to spend time with you and since I know you can cook but you've got your hands full with the farm right now, let me take care of it. You'll get it next time."

A jab to his heart made him wonder when the next time would be. He was going to be leaving soon and picnics weren't something that was a weekday kind of thing, unless it was at the farm, and then he'd be shirking his responsibility at the ranch, despite what Dad said about firing him and getting back in the saddle.

He could see the smile quirk the corners of her mouth in the soft streetlamp light.

"If you insist, who am I to argue. But can you actually cook? You can't just run down to a gourmet store and order a picnic basket to go; we're not in Dallas."

He chuckled. "Now you're getting on board and don't you worry. I've actually learned how to cook quite well, and I promise you won't go hungry and everything will taste good."

"After a day in the field, I'll be starving."

He opened the passenger door for her and waited until she got in before leaning in. "Renee, this has been the best three days I've had in a very long time and I'm going to have to give the cattle an extra ration of oats as thanks for helping us reconnect."

She tipped her head. "When you put it that way, I guess it has been a pretty happy accident that the fence was down and they braved the river to find greener grass on the other side."

He cupped her cheek in his hand and lowered his lips to hers. "Sometimes old sayings are true." His lips lingered on hers; he was not ready for the evening to be over.

"What sayings aren't true?"

"That you can't go home again." He looked into her eyes. "Coming home, so many things are the same and the best unexpected surprise of all was you."

"I feel the same way. Seeing you has been wonderful."

He could see the shutters roll down over her emotions as soon as the words left her mouth. The but was left unspoken and dangling. Unwilling to tear down what they had begun to rediscover, he said, "Let's make our plans and stay in the moment. The future isn't important right now. I just want to spend time with you."

She brushed the hair from his forehead. "Next week will come, but you're right; I don't want to think about it. I want to enjoy this time with you. I'm alive again. It's as if I've been living in some kind of gray haze and you've brought brilliant color back to me."

She said it perfectly. His fog lifted and he was seeing life much more clearly. Not that he was ready to make any declaration, but he did have time to make plans.

"My life is better when you're in it, Renee." He kissed her one more time, slow and sweet, before it was time to drive her home.

9

$\mathcal{R}$enee lay in her cozy bed and ran a finger over her lips. Looking out the window, the early morning sky was a pale gray and the sun would be inching upward soon, but all she wanted to do was think of last night and the way it felt to be in Hank's arms and taste his sweet kisses on her lips. Memories washed over her, back to a time when their love was fresh and heart-pounding. Time spent with him was like nothing she had ever experienced since, and last night was a reminder of all the feelings she had worked so hard to suppress. But now she knew love wasn't something to forget but to treasure, and even if nothing ever went any further between them, at least she remembered what it was like to love the one man she never forgot.

Her phone rang and she looked at caller ID. "How did you know I was thinking of you?"

Hank's low, smooth laugh caused a butterfly explosion in her stomach. How could that happen with just a laugh?

"I didn't wake you?"

"No, I was thinking about what a nice time I had last

night." No way was she going to confess she had been thinking about the past. Living in the moment was all they really had.

"I was wondering if you had plans for today?"

Her pulse quickened. Just the suggestion of plans had her sitting up straight. "I need to check on the new plantings and walk the fence line. Call it being a little overly cautious, but I want to make sure nothing toppled over."

"Are you questioning the skill of the people who set the posts yesterday?"

She could hear the playful mocking in his voice. "You know that I've always been the one to double- and triple-check everything. Why should the fence be any different?"

"True. Care for some company?"

He couldn't keep hanging out at the farm; he had things to do at Stones Throw Ranch. She wanted to say yes, but she didn't want to put him in a time crunch either. It was like that as teenagers. He'd get up early and rush through his chores just to spend time with her.

"I'd like that, but I've taken up a lot of your time for the last few days with all my problems, of which you've solved most of them. Thank you again." She took a moment to slow her breathing. "But if you want to do something later, maybe we could meet for a quick lunch at the river. I'd be happy to do that."

"Oh, I thought since last night and all, you'd want to spend more time together."

Even though he stopped speaking, it felt like the thought continued with, *I'll be leaving soon.* She was an adult and she could handle him leaving again. *Yeah, right.*

"I get it. You think I have stuff to get done here." He paused. "Dad fired me yesterday. Told me I was done filling in for him at the ranch so I'm at loose ends for the next couple of days."

Her heart soared and it didn't matter that he sort of indicated he had time before he went back to Dallas. They'd be able to spend time together and who knows? Maybe they could try something long distance. It wasn't like she had met anyone else she wanted to date and some time with Hank was better than zero time with him. "In that case, do you want to head over in about an hour? We'll check out the new fields and I'll play hooky for the rest of the day."

"Now you're talking." His voice got a little amped. "And we can do anything you want today. So give it some thought."

"I will." She laughed softly. "See you soon."

She flung back the blanket and her feet hit the cool pine floor. The reflection in the mirror was the girl she remembered; deep-red hair framed her face with a few fine lines around her eyes—smile lines is what Mom called them— and a smattering of light freckles sure to deepen in the coming summer months. She was a few pounds heavier than in college, but she'd worked hard to not get too curvy. It wasn't a vanity thing but for good health and now that she was actually working outside all day, she was seeing muscle definition that hadn't been there in years. Even if she'd been around the sun more times than she wanted to count, it was pretty obvious Hank still found her attractive.

Time hadn't hurt him one bit. He was lean and muscular, but it was his kindness that she always thought of first and second was his caramel-brown eyes.

She hurried into the kitchen and brewed a small pot of coffee before checking the forecast and email. The delivery of parts for the cider press were due tomorrow which was a good thing since they needed to finish that project before moving on to the next broken machine. It was never-ending but she had taken the farm on with enthusiasm despite the challenges she might face. This had always been her plan. It had taken a few years longer to build up her savings to make the leap.

The crunch of tires on stone drew her attention. It had to be Hank, but he was ahead of schedule. She stepped out onto the porch. An unfamiliar dark SUV parked, its windows darkened with that special film that gave people inside privacy and protected them from the hot sun. It was something she'd expect to see anywhere but River Junction. They must have taken a wrong turn somewhere along the road, but she'd get them headed in the right direction within minutes.

The driver got out and opened the back door. An older man, who might be pushing sixty, got out and looked around. With the time it took him, she knew he had taken in everything—the peeling paint on the barn, the age of the tractor parked under the lean-to roof, and the house which too had seen better days. Her back stiffened. New trees came before cosmetic touches. Finally, he turned and acknowledged her with a slight nod. She strode down the steps to where the man stood.

"Hello, may I help you?"

"Ms. Mitchell, it's a pleasure to meet you. I'm Lucas Gasperini." He extended his hand and gave hers a limp shake. "I'm pleased to discover you're home today. I've dropped in a couple of times only to discover you've been out."

She wasn't about to tell him she would have been working. She stuck her hands in her jeans pockets and kept her face neutral. "I was unaware. How can I help you?" It was unnerving to know he had been on her property before.

"I'd like to buy your farm and it's my understanding you're the sole owner since your parents retired."

She was trying desperately to remember if her parents had mentioned his name, but she was coming up blank. "You want to buy my farm, but it's not for sale."

"A minor detail." He handed her a piece of paper. "As you can see, my offer is quite generous and it would give you an opportunity to purchase a lovely home and live very comfortably."

She glanced at the number and then looked again. There were digits that she hadn't ever seen coupled together on a farm offer. Not that she wanted to sell her family's home, but she had a moment of pause. "This is an amazing offer but why do you want to purchase my orchard?"

"You misunderstand. It's not the orchard I'm interested in acquiring. I'll have the orchards removed but the land is more valuable to me with its mineral rights."

He stated it so matter-of-factly it was almost underwhelming.

"Of course, there is much work to discover what is actually here but based on early reports, it has significant potential and I want to buy it before anyone else has the chance to stake a claim."

"Mr. Gasperini, thank you for your interest but Riverbend isn't for sale. I'm sure you understand, and as far as mineral rights are concerned, I'm surprised you were so forthcoming with why you want the land."

"In my line of work, I've discovered brutally honest is the only way to conduct business. If I had convinced you to sell your farm and you found out after the fact, well, that would sully my reputation and that's just something that would be intolerable."

Renee was relieved to see Hank's truck lumber up the drive. After all, he was a lawyer and he'd be able to help her convince this man she had no interest in his offer.

She held up her hand with a wave. "Hank."

Mr. Gasperini turned and looked him up and down. He seemed to take note of his dusty boots, faded jeans, red plaid shirt, and tan cowboy hat.

He closed the distance between them and touched the back of her arm, giving it a light squeeze of support away from prying eyes of the stranger. "Renee, I didn't realize you were expecting anyone this morning."

His words were carefully measured, and she guessed this was how the lawyer in him sounded.

"I wasn't. Mr. Gasperini arrived and stated he's been here recently before this morning, and in fact, he just offered to buy the farm from me." She handed him the slip of paper with the dollar figure.

His face never changed. "Mr. Gasperini, I'm sure Ms. Mitchell has told you her orchard isn't for sale and there are other larger orchards which might be a better investment."

With a dismissive wave of his hand, he said, "I don't give a fig about the orchard; in fact, I detest anything apple. My interest is the land." He waved his hand around. "All of this would be bulldozed."

Renee clasped her hands in front of her. "Hank, he's interested in mineral rights."

He gave her a side-look. "And what was your

response? Is this something we should discuss?" He stuck out his hand to Mr. Gasperini. "Hank Shepard, I'm Ms. Mitchell's attorney."

His eyes widened for a fraction of a second, and if Renee hadn't been watching, she would have missed it.

"I was about to tell Mr. Gasperini my home is not for sale, at any price."

He gave a brisk nod. "You could check around with other family-owned businesses, but I think you'll find most people around here aren't quick to part with a living legacy."

"You would pass up on a very comfortable early retirement?" Mr. Gasperini's gaze never left her.

"I'm not ready to give up on my dream and challenges. I'm proud to be a small, woman-owned business." She held out her hand and gave his a firm shake. "Thank you for your interest but no thanks."

If anyone thought she was a pushover, they'd better think again. If there was one thing she knew from growing up here, it was that Montana could chew you up and spit you out. Heck, that had been the same when she was in Chicago, but this was different. River Junction was her home and she wasn't going to sell no matter how much money someone offered her.

Mr. Gasperini took a few steps to the SUV door and paused. Looking at her with a steady glare, he said, "You could name your price, you know."

She lifted her chin and never blinked. "My home is priceless."

He tipped his head to one side before getting in the vehicle. As fast as he came, he left. She exhaled the breath she didn't know she had been holding. "Can you believe that guy?"

Hank slipped an arm around her waist and held her close to his side. If he could feel her shaking, he didn't mention it. "You were amazing. Other people would have given that amount of money a second and third thought before turning him down flat."

"Would you sell off Stone's Throw Ranch for a big payday?"

Without a moment's hesitation, he said, "Absolutely not. Three generations of Shepards have worked hard to make the ranch what it is today. Selling out would mean their work was for nothing."

He understood where she was coming from. But if that was the case, why didn't he want to stay? He was a mass of contradictions.

"Now that we've had our excitement for the day, are you ready for boring?"

He dropped his lips to hers. "I can't wait. Time with you is never boring."

10

———————

ank walked alongside Renee, holding her hand as they inspected the fence line. He didn't doubt everything would be exactly as they had left it, but he was with the only woman he had ever loved and it didn't matter what she wanted to do. By her side was the only place he wanted to be. And now that his dad fired him from working at the ranch, he had nothing to do but think about his future. Maybe that was all part of Dad's plan.

He was a lawyer and he passed the bar in Montana, but would practicing law in his hometown be fulfilling? Writing wills or reviewing real estate transactions were not exactly what he thought his future would hold. But he had to admit his life was an empty shell in Texas and it didn't matter if he tried to convince himself a long-distance relationship would work. Talking on the phone, texting, or video calls would never fill the void.

Their fingers were intertwined, and the warmth from her hand filled his heart in a way that he hadn't felt in years. Wasn't this what life should be about, walking hand in hand with the woman you loved, doing mundane things that seemed like perfection?

She gave him a sidelong look. "What are you thinking about? You have a silly smile on your face, kind of like you got the last piece of huckleberry pie at Maggie's diner."

He lifted her hand and kissed the back of it. "I was thinking how it doesn't matter what we do. As long as we're together, I'm happy."

Her face softened and her eyes misted over. She had always been tenderhearted and that was just one of the many qualities he loved about her.

She now gave him a quizzical look. "I'll have to admit I'm confused." They continued to walk at a leisurely pace, but she wasn't looking at the fence or him. "What are we doing? I mean, don't get me wrong, I love being with you, but it's stirred up feelings I thought were long gone and what happens when you leave? I'm not looking for fluffy romantic promises, but do we agree to enjoy what we have now and stay friends, keep in touch with the occasional phone call or email, and exchange cards on holidays? Is that what you're thinking?"

The air was sucked from his lungs. How could she think this was just some kind of an interlude and not the real deal between them? "That was a lot of questions, but would you prefer that we just keep our relationship as friendly and not explore what the possibilities might be?"

"Hank, that's completely illogical. We live fifteen hundred miles apart; it's not like we'll be getting together on weekends after a couple hours of windshield time."

He stopped walking and stepped in front of her to take both her hands in his. "This last week with you has shown me one thing; I have never stopped loving you. You're the beat of my heart and without you in my life I'm like the

Tin Man. You brought the sunlight and stars back into a dull-gray existence, and it took coming home and having some cows lead me back to you to see the truth."

He could see confusion cloud her eyes and he understood how she felt. He'd been wrestling with this for the last twenty-four plus hours. "I thought we could hang out and be friends, just like when we were kids. Have some fun and enjoy spending time together but I have to be honest and ask if you feel the same?"

"Are you asking me if I want to have a long-distance relationship?" She walked a few paces down the path and looked out over the freshly planted trees.

"Yes, I am. I don't want us to lose contact again and at least until we figure out a longer-term solution, I want us to talk and see each other when we can. I can see about working remotely when I don't have to be in court, maybe some long weekends over the next few months. It's not ideal but at the very least it's a start."

Pulling her hands away, she walked a short distance before stopping. His heart hammered in his chest; he wanted her to say it's what she wanted too.

"It won't be easy, and I've had friends who tried the long-distance thing and it didn't work so instead of putting boundaries around whatever we might have, instead we should agree we're going to work on our friendship and see where it goes."

It wasn't exactly what he had in mind, especially since kissing her and holding her in his arms was not a friend kind of a thing, but if that was all she was willing to offer, then he'd accept her terms. In a few long strides he was next to her. "Renee, if that's what you want, then that's what we'll do."

She threw her arms around his neck and hugged him

tight. "Don't misunderstand. I have strong feelings for you but I'm scared to death I'll get hurt again and I couldn't bear it. Losing us once was painful; losing us twice would be excruciating."

He inhaled the sweetness of her vanilla shampoo and sun-dried clothes. This was his Montana memory and one he'd carry with him on the plane home. A lump lodged in his throat. How was he going to get through every day without seeing her, holding her? It had been less than a week and each morning he woke up looking forward to seeing her smile. He held her a little tighter until she said, "Are you trying to commit this moment to just a memory or can we get back to our walk?"

The lightness in her tone didn't hide the emotion in her words. He relaxed his arms and placed a kiss on her temple. She felt so right in his arms he wasn't ready to let her go.

"Let's finish work so we can spend more time having fun. I was thinking we could go for a trail ride later and maybe an early dinner."

"That sounds nice." She cupped his cheek in her hand. "You are a very special man, Hank Shepard, and no matter what happens between us, I'm glad we've had this time together."

Throwing a saddle blanket over the back of one of the mares, Renee called out, "What's her name again?"

With a chuckle, he said, "Dolly and she's partial to apples, not so much carrots."

He came out of the tack room with a saddle for his

gelding and set it on the saddle stand before getting the saddle Renee would use.

She stared at what Hank held in his hands and her mouth gaped. "You still have my saddle?"

It was the one he had bought for her when she was sixteen, hand tooled flowers with an intricate basket weave pattern. The seat was padded suede adorned with silver conchos and silver plates. She had always said it was a work of art.

"Of course. I would never get rid of it." He placed it on Dolly's back and tightened the girth strap.

"I figured it was long gone." She ran her fingertips over the tooled roses as if she were seeing it for the first time. "I always wondered…"

She didn't finish the sentence but he knew. He had often thought he should have dropped it by her parents' place. They had horses too, but this had been their special thing to do at his parents' ranch, saddle up and ride. The only downside was the mounts they used to ride have long since gone over the rainbow bridge, but he would never have gotten rid of her saddle. In his heart he dreamed he'd ride with Renee again and now it was coming true.

They finished getting the horses ready when he heard his mom's voice calling to them.

"In the barn," he yelled over his shoulder.

She entered carrying a basket. "Hello, you two. I thought you'd like to take a light supper with you."

"Hi, Maeve. That wasn't necessary. I don't think we'll be gone long."

"Hold on. I'll get a saddle bag to carry everything." He stepped into the tack room, leaving the two women. He could hear Renee thank his mom for everything. He paused, giving them another moment when their voices dropped too low for him to hear. Curious, he went back in.

"Are you two sharing secrets about this handsome rancher?" He gave Renee an exaggerated wink.

"Someone thinks very highly of himself." Mom gave Renee a one-armed hug. "Good luck, Renee; his head might not fit through the barn door."

"Mom." He held his hand up. "Family loyalty."

"Son, sometimes the truth is too important to hide it." She fluttered her fingers as she walked out the door, laughing as she slid it closed.

Once the saddle bags were secured in place on Ranger's backside, they walked the horses outside. The sun was headed toward the horizon. It was going to be a spectacular trail ride. The sky was clear, the air was cool, and there would be a full moon tonight. Originally Hank thought it was the perfect night for romance but given their conversation earlier, he'd have to play it cool and not put any pressure on her.

Holding Dolly's reins, Renee swung a leg up and over and leaned over the mare's neck to whisper in her ear. She grinned at him. "We're just getting acquainted before we spend time together."

He mounted Ranger and settled in with a light tap of his heels. The quarter horse moved to the open gate. Dolly walked beside him and by the smile on Renee's face, she was already having a good time. Once they cleared the gate, the horses eased into a trot and it was easy to see that Renee hadn't lost her grace in the saddle.

She flashed him a grin, adjusted her cowboy hat, and tapped her heels to the mare who broke into a light lope. Her deep-red hair flowing in the breeze, her musical laughter reached his ears. Tonight was just what they needed.

Once they reached a stand of pines, they pulled the horses up and dismounted, looping the reins around a low branch.

She rubbed Dolly's neck. "This is a great spot. We can watch the stars when they put in an appearance."

He gave her a gentle shoulder bump. "I'm holding out for the moonlight."

Color flushed high in her cheeks. She pulled a blanket roll from the back of her saddle and flicked it out to cover the scrubby grass. "Are you building a fire?"

"Of course. Help me gather some wood?" He held out his hand to her and he was pleased she took it without hesitation.

After they had gathered enough wood for a decent fire, he got it going. The air was already cooling off. He could offer to keep her warm, but he remembered his promise to himself not to push her too hard or too fast.

With the fire crackling and remnants of dinner spread out around them, they reclined on the blanket. The moon began its ascent in the sky. It seemed like they had already run out of things to say, but he had much to talk about. "I was thinking about when we were kids and the first time our dads let us go on an evening trail ride." He covered her hand and gave it a squeeze. "Do you remember?"

She laughed. "Dad was at the ranch when we got back with the flimsy excuse that he needed to talk about a load of manure for our garden. Like we needed a whole honey wagon full."

"I do remember that and when I said I was driving you home, the look on their faces was priceless, like you were going to end our date being driven home by your dad."

"After that I guess they figured we knew what we were

doing riding after dark, but wow, they were so transparent." She leaned in and kissed his cheek. "Tonight, our fathers won't be waiting for us."

She was breathtaking as the growing moonlight graced her skin. "Oh good, then taking you home won't be a problem." He lowered his lips to hers.

11

*R*enee looked at the clock, wishing that time would slow to a crawl, at least for today. It was Hank's final morning, and they were going to spend it together before he headed to Bozeman to catch his night flight back to Dallas. Last night had been wonderful but in looking back at the last week, every minute with him had been special and she wished she'd known he was in town weeks ago. However, the circumstances of them reconnecting was something organic, natural after all this time and totally unexpected in the best way possible.

Hank was sitting in the truck, staring straight ahead. He looked as if he'd lost his best friend. Her gut tightened as she watched him from the kitchen, and she knew how he must be feeling since that thought had crossed her mind several times this morning. She put a smile on her face. Life was better when you had someone special in your life, especially a man like Hank Shepard, no matter how fleeting.

She didn't rush out the door but watched him from the

kitchen until he pushed open the door on the truck. Taking her time, she crossed the room to the back door.

His eyes lit up when they met hers and his steps quickened, reaching her in a few long strides. He pulled her into his arms and held her close. She felt him take several slow, deep breaths, then he ran his fingertips down the curve of her cheeks and traced her lips before his touched hers.

She savored the feel of his kiss, missing it and him already. Easing back, she said, "Are you all packed?"

He nodded and said, "Louis is going to drive me to the airport. Dad's been feeling pretty good, but I don't think he should make the drive to Bozeman. It's a long time to be sitting when he's just starting to get more comfortable with walking."

"I can see where you're coming from; maybe your next trip out." Her breath caught. They hadn't talked about when he was coming back to Montana, and she wanted to ask but didn't want to appear clingy and needy.

Slinging an arm around her shoulders, he steered her to the porch. "We have a couple of hours. What do you want to do? Walk, horseback ride, ATVs? Just name it."

"Let's walk down to the river and make sure the cows are staying on their side."

He gave a wide-eyed stare. "We fixed the fence." And then he grinned. "I see what you're doing, just poking at me." He pulled her closer and kissed her forehead. "I'm going to miss this."

Softly, she said, "Me too." She took his hand and they strolled in the direction of the field before she changed and headed to the barn. "I want to show you something." It was an idea she'd had buzzing around her head, and she decided to bounce it off him.

They entered the dimly lit barn with the sun at their backs. Leaving the doors wide open, she crossed to an interior room. She flicked the light and on shelves were rows of jars with bright-red labels. The writing couldn't be seen from the doorway. She gave him a small smile. Would he think this was a dumb idea? He was the first person she'd shared it with.

"I was thinking of expanding besides the pick your own apples and cider for the fall season. I found my grandmother's apple butter and caramel apple jam recipes so last year I made some. This is sort of my testing lab to see how they hold up to storage."

He crossed the room and picked up a jar. He turned to look at her. "Have you been holding out on me? I had no idea you made this kind of stuff."

She chuckled. "Don't get too excited; you haven't tried it yet."

"Crackers, biscuits, or heck, just a spoon will work." He picked up a jar and waved it toward the door. "Lead the way to the kitchen." He grabbed another jar so now he had one of each.

She wanted to dance her way across the driveway, thrilled he hadn't said the idea was a bad one and he wanted to try them. She'd been eating it all winter and it was holding up perfectly.

The old-fashioned kitchen suddenly felt cozy with Hank in it. She gestured to the table. "Make yourself comfortable."

He pulled out two chairs and took one. "I've always liked this house; it's always felt like my second home."

She glanced over her shoulder as she pulled a box of crackers from the cupboard. "You spent enough time here growing up."

"That's what happens when your childhood friend morphs into the girl next door."

He winked and her pulse quickened. Not one to cry over what might have been but instead celebrate what was happening in the moment, she crossed the room and plunked down. The jars were opened, and she placed the crackers on paper towels.

She placed a hand on his. "Now you have to promise to be honest. If you don't like one or both, you have to tell me. I want to expand what I can sell and longer term even have a mail order business if it takes off."

"I like that you're thinking about the future."

He scooped up the apple butter first and slathered the cracker so Renee could only see the apple mixture and popped it in his mouth. He closed his eyes and chewed very slowly.

She jabbed him in the side. "It's not like you have to chew your food for a minute before swallowing."

Without commenting, he repeated the process with another cracker. Only this time she saw the twinkle in his eyes. "Hank, come on, tell me what you think."

He wiped the crumbs from the corner of his mouth. "It's very good."

She waited for him to elaborate and when he didn't, she jabbed his side again. He laughed again.

"What was that for?"

"It's good, is that it?" She had played with a combination of cinnamon and nutmeg to try and mimic the flavors of apple pie and in each batch, she had used a different variety of apples. This particular one was a blend to achieve a sweetness without adding sugar. After all that tinkering, she thought it was perfect.

"You're impatient today. But just relax and I'll tell you what I think after I try the jam."

After about five minutes of Hank testing and re-tasting each jar several times, he grinned.

"I can't tell you which one is my favorite; I love the complexity of the apple butter with the spices and richness of the apple texture, but then the jam has the flavor of a great caramel apple without the stickiness that comes with it. Did you create these recipes yourself or use ones your mom had?"

"No, remember I said before these were my grand-mother's. I started with her basic idea and then after making multiple batches of each, these were my favorites. I sent a couple of jars of all my batches to my parents, just to see what they think, and they agreed these were their favorites too."

"Where do you go from here? Have you written a business plan for the expansion of your business?"

He always was the practical one; she was the dreamer. But she had, in fact, created a plan and started to look into costs to install a commercial kitchen and processing right down to staffing needs. All that was left to do was pull the trigger.

"I have and even though it will take a year to get the commercial space built, I want to start later in the season after I approach a few of the stores in town to see if they'd sell jars and maybe even Maggie would serve them at the diner and offer jars for sale to her customers. Tourism is growing in this part of the state, and I'd like to think people would buy jars to take home with them, hence online sales might grow even more once people have tried it."

"I'd be happy to look over any contracts for you and

you should have a basic form for any business that is accepting your product on consignment or straight-up purchase for resale."

Now this wasn't why she brought it up to get free legal advice. "That's not necessary." She could hear the frosty edge in her voice, and she toned it back. "But thank you."

"Think of it as my way of helping you and you can pay me in all the apple butter and jam I can eat." He stroked her cheek. "Renee, I care for you a great deal and if I can help in some small way, I'd like for you to think about accepting the offer. I want to see your business grow and this is a great concept. You could also produce other products to offer, maybe beauty products down the road, develop an entire line."

That was an interesting idea. "I'd need a chemist for that."

He grabbed his phone. "Okay to tap into your network?"

She gave him the password and wondered what he was going to look up. It didn't take long before he turned the phone so she could scan the article on the screen.

She was surprised to see there were recipes online for creams, face masks, and more that all used apples as the main ingredient. She took the phone and her breath caught. Was this a real possibility? "Do you really think I can expand into something like this?"

"With a plan and timeline, you can do anything with the orchard. I know your parents have agreements with some companies for apples, but we live in an area where there is a lot of open space and I'm sure if you needed to expand you could."

"We still have a lot of acreage that isn't planted." She began to make a mental list of things to do after Hank left, and then as quickly as it started, she pushed it aside. "I can work on that later; we only have a short time left before you're leaving."

He circled the air in front of her face with his hand. "I can tell your wheels are spinning. Get a pad and write down your ideas and you can go back to them later. Keep pushing yourself and bounce all the ideas you want off me but first concentrate on the low-hanging fruit."

She laughed. "I see what you did there."

"Jams, jellies, and the apple butter for year one, beyond that push yourself further. But make a plan and then execute it."

She moved from her chair to his lap and slid her arms around his neck. Looking deep into his eyes, she could see he really was being supportive and that validated her ideas; not that she needed it from him, but she was glad to have it all the same.

"Change of plans. How about instead of walking around, we stay right here in each other's arms until you have to leave. I want to be able to close my eyes and feel your arms around me after you've gone."

He nibbled her lips. "You're making this very hard to leave."

She longed for time to stop and put a bubble around them. "I'm not trying to be difficult but now that we've found each other again, it puts a different spin on time together. Each minute is precious."

He placed his forehead against hers. "I'm going to miss you like crazy too."

12

---

*H*ank had his feet propped on his oversized walnut desk. He loosened his tie and ran a hand over his crew cut. It had been a brutal day and he'd only been back a week. He was missing the ranch pace but even more he was lost without Renee. The quick texts, phone calls, and video chats just weren't enough, and he kept wondering what he was doing in Dallas when the woman he loved was fifteen hundred miles away.

His cell buzzed with an incoming call. "Hey, Mom." He plowed ahead without waiting for her to speak. "Is everything okay at the house?"

"It is. I just wanted to check on my youngest son to see how you were doing, being back in the big city and all."

He looked out the window. His view was spectacular from the tenth floor and his office building was on the outskirts of the city so he overlooked the crowded suburbs.

"It's business as usual." But it wasn't at all like it had been three months ago, before going back to Montana and reconnecting with Renee. He realized how empty his life had become, not the success in his professional life but in all the ways that mattered.

"You have that distant tone in your voice again. I was hoping coming home would have pushed that into the past."

His mom's voice wasn't harsh; she was just stating a fact as she saw it. He wanted to unburden himself to her, but her advice would be to pack up and make the long drive home. A part of him wanted to do just that but doubts lingered.

"Hank, do you want to talk about what's weighing heavy on your heart?"

And just like that she'd cut to the core of the problem. "It's okay. I just had a long day." Anxious to change the subject, he asked, "How's Dad doing?"

"Happy to be back in the saddle."

"I thought he wasn't supposed to ride for a couple more weeks." His father was a stubborn man but that was just foolhardy.

"He's not literally riding a horse but zipping around in the UTV, keeping track of things, and I haven't seen him this happy in a long time."

He sighed. "You had me worried for a second. I know Dad's surgery was from a fall and if the doctor hasn't released him to ride yet, I didn't want him to slide backward."

"He's behaving for a change even if it pains him to do so."

A sliver of concern snaked down his back. Neither him nor his brother were there to keep a handle on the ranch. Maybe that too was a mistake.

"Have you heard from Ford recently?"

"A week or so ago. I think he's having trouble with

Sharon. She never seems to be home and he has his hands full with Toby asking for his mommy."

Living in Tennessee couldn't be easy, but like everyone, Ford needed to find his own path. "That's rough, but he'll figure out what he needs to do. Maybe I'll give him a call and see if they want to come home for the holidays. Toby can miss preschool and Ford gets laid off at the end of the year so an extended stay might be just what they need."

"Does that mean you're coming home too?"

The hopeful tone in her voice constricted his heart. He had spent too many years working through the holidays so other lawyers with kids could have extra time off, but his family had suffered too.

"I plan on being home and a few long weekends before then."

His mom grew quiet.

"Mom, are you okay if I come home more?" He heard her sniff and he felt like a jerk; he hadn't meant to make her cry.

"The door is always open and the coffee's always on."

A smile spread across his face and he wished he was walking in the old wooden door right now. "Mom, have I told you lately that you're the best mother for me?"

"I've had some experience and since I've just gotten a huge kudos, I have to ask, what's going on with you and Renee? I saw her at the post office the other day and she was looking kind of down in the mouth."

That didn't make him feel good to know she was sad, but it was just one more reason to really think about what he was going to do next. He knew her parents weren't back from New Mexico yet. "Mom, do me a favor. Ask her to come for dinner on Sunday. All she does is work and I'm pretty sure she couldn't say no to some of your home cooking. Maybe even mention you'll make that cake she loves so much."

"I'll call her tomorrow and let you know what she said."

An idea was starting to form. "Don't tell her I suggested it, and let me know what time you're eating so I can call and talk to you all at the same time."

After he said goodbye to his mom, he drafted a letter to his boss and sent it via email. Next, he pulled up his caseload and prioritized what he needed to finish up before he left for the day. Sunday was only six days away and he had a lot to wrap up.

*L*ife was a whirlwind of activity over the next four days and Hank had no idea how he had gotten everything done but he was in the driver's seat of his SUV and ready hit to the highway. In the predawn light the sun promised another scorcher. The back was packed with boxes. He had a cooler on the passenger seat, tunes on the radio, and the Dallas skyline was in his rearview mirror. He was going home and with some luck, he'd get there in time for Sunday dinner at five.

After a few hours on the road, he stopped for hot coffee and called his brother. They still needed to talk about the holidays.

"Hey, Ford, got a couple of minutes to talk to your little brother?"

"Well, I just dropped Toby off for a playdate, so yeah, I've got some time to spare." He paused. "Where are you? That's not office sounds in the background."

He chuckled and scanned the landscape in front of him. "I'm almost into New Mexico."

"What are you talking about? You're usually in the office this time of day."

He tightened his hands on the steering wheel. "Not today." No way was he going to tell him exactly what was going on. It would ruin his surprise. "Just taking a little day trip."

"Good, you work too hard; hopefully there's a lady involved."

Hank skipped that comment and instead launched into his idea about the holidays. "Mom and Dad would be thrilled to have you and Toby from before Thanksgiving until after the new year. What do you say?" He didn't bother to pretend to include Sharon in the plans; he was pretty sure she was out of the picture.

"I'll give it some thought."

Even though Ford couldn't see him, he was nodding. "Good, well, I hope you'll give it some serious thought; it'd mean a lot to Mom and Dad, and Toby will have a blast, cutting down a tree and Santa's reindeer on the roof."

"All good times for sure."

Hank wanted his nephew to have good old-fashioned Montana holidays like they had as kids and who knows? Maybe Ford would decide it was a better place for them both.

"It's a good idea and I'll think it over. Can I let you know in a few days?"

The unspoken question weighed heavy on Hank. "Yeah, of course, and bro, are you doing okay?"

"Some days are better than others, but we will be."

The sheen on his happiness dimmed a little when he heard his brother force out the sentence.

"Thanks for calling, Hank, and we'll talk soon."

"Sounds good, and Ford, and if want to talk, you know how to reach me." He ended the call and the miles slipped away.

State lines came and went. When he was growing close to Wyoming, his eyelids were becoming weighted and he pulled into a motel for the night. He was making good time and after a decent night's sleep, he'd hit the road again.

After an uneventful drive through Wyoming, signs for Montana welcomed him home. A few more hours and the next phase of his life would begin.

*H*ank stopped the SUV at the end of his parents' driveway. The windows were down and he took a few moments to take in the sweet fresh air of home. He could see Renee's pickup parked in the driveway and in a few minutes she'd be in his arms. He eased forward and parked out of view of the house and made the rest of his trip on foot. His hand rested on the doorknob, and he turned it quietly, savoring the anticipation of the surprise. Heart hammering in his chest, he touched his chest pocket.

Strolling into the kitchen, he was disappointed they weren't sitting at the table, but voices from the dining room drifted his way. He moved into the next room and hovered in the doorway. Renee was sitting with her back to him, long waves of deep-red hair cascading down her back. Mom looked up and her mouth forward a small O. Dad's eyes grew wide, and Hank cleared his throat.

"Do you have enough for one more?"

Renee turned in the chair, then got up and leaped into his arms, covering his face with kisses.

Her hands were on either side of his cheeks and confusion filled her eyes. "What are you doing here?"

"I heard Mom was making pot roast and those little potatoes I like, and I just can't get a decent meal in Dallas so here I am." He grinned and then pulled her to his chest, and for her ears alone, asked, "Nice surprise?"

With a sob caught in her throat, she said, "Yes."

Mom and Dad watched the reunion and he held out his hand for them to stay put. He had something to say and wanted them to hear it.

He eased her from his arms. "Renee, the last two weeks have been torture, and I knew the minute I stepped on the plane that I was making a mistake, but it took me some time to make things right."

Holding her right hand in his, he dropped to one knee and withdrew a diamond ring from his shirt pocket. "I hope you'll forgive me for taking so long to ask you a very important question, but I know where I want to be and who I want to be with."

Her free hand covered her trembling lips and she blinked tears from her eyes.

"Renee Mitchell, will you agree to marry me and live the rest of our lives in our hometown?"

She dropped to her knees. "Hank, are you sure you want to leave Dallas?"

"Darlin', I already have. The condo's been listed; I resigned from the firm, and all that I wanted to keep is in the back of my SUV. So, marry me and make me the happiest man on earth."

She tenderly kissed his lips and she wiped away the dampness on his cheeks. "I'll marry you on one condition."

"Name it, my love."

She tipped her head. "I want us to get married during apple blossom time next spring."

He threw his head back and laughed, and then he kissed her again. "Under the apple blossoms in Montana it is."

EPILOGUE

Spring the Following Year

*R*enee smoothed her hand over her ivory lace bodice. The last year had been a whirlwind filled with fun, laughter, and love, and today Hank would be waiting for her in the apple orchard among the trees they had planted last spring. They would start their future together as husband and wife where this new romance had begun but sans the cattle.

She leaned into the mirror and checked her pale-pink lipstick. Her brown eyes seemed huge, enhanced by the artfully applied makeup. It was sweet that Mom had insisted a professional hair and makeup artist come to the house for the day. She wanted to go out and triple-check that everything was set for the reception in the main barn, but she couldn't take the chance that Hank would see her roaming around. Instead, she closed her eyes and pictured the transformation. White gauzy fabric created a cozy inti-mate feel; clear twinkle lights were everywhere, and soon it would be filled with their friends and family celebrating their special day.

The door eased open with a soft tap. She turned to see Mom and Dad all dressed up in their wedding finery, holding hands. Dad was in his tuxedo with a pink apple blossom corsage in his lapel and her mother looked beautiful in a deep-green gown, the perfect shade reminiscent of leaves on the apple trees.

"Sweetheart." Mom stepped into the room. "The buggy is out front. Are you ready to find your groom?"

She pressed her hand to her midsection but that did nothing to quiet her nerves. "Why am I so nervous?"

"Today's the day you've been waiting for ever since you were a little girl. Even when you were small and played wedding, you'd call that large teddy bear that you used as your groom, Hank. You always knew he was the only man for you."

She smiled and wrapped her arms around Mom. "He's an amazing guy and we're going to do great things with this farm, you wait and see. I'll make you proud."

Dad wrapped his arms around both of the women. "We don't have to wait, honey; you already have, and Hank is darn lucky to be marrying you today."

Renee blinked away the tears that sprang to her eyes. There was no way she had time to get her makeup fixed and she didn't want to keep her soon-to-be husband waiting.

"Thanks, Dad, for everything, your support, guidance, and for trusting me—well, us now—with the orchard."

"I was surprised when he wanted to be a farmer instead of a rancher but whatever makes you two happy is what makes me happy."

She hugged her dad tight. "Thanks, Dad."

• • •

*H*ank stood under the arbor in the middle of the apple orchard, his hands clasped in front of him. The timing couldn't have been more perfect. The trees were blossoming; the new trees were growing, and the weather was mild. It was the perfect day to marry the only woman he had ever loved.

He scanned the guests and it warmed his heart to see most of the town's residents of River Junction had come to share this day with him and Renee. His parents were in the front row, his brother, Ford, was by his side as his best man. The wedding march swelled from the portable speakers, and Renee, with her mom on one side and her dad on the other, began the walk down the path that led to him.

His breath caught. She was so beautiful. The long ivory gown swished around her legs as she walked. He could see the glow on her face and her soft-brown eyes were filled with love. It seemed to take forever for her to reach him so he took two steps forward, his eyes locked on hers.

She stretched out her hand to him and he clasped it, warmth spreading over him.

He kissed her cheek. "Hi. I've been waiting for you." This was their day.

She laughed softly. "I hope I'm worth the wait."

They stepped before the minister and for her ears alone, he said, "I would have waited for this day for all eternity, but I'm glad I didn't have to."

The ceremony was a blur, but they recited each vow in a clear voice. There was no place he'd rather be than holding his bride's hand in the orchard.

The minster said the final blessing and then the words he had been waiting for. "Hank, you may kiss your wife."

He leaned in close and before his lips touched hers, he said, "I'll love you forever, my beautiful orchard bride." They sealed their future with a kiss.

The End
Keep reading for the next Orchard Bride Book
Falling for Paige Under The Peach Tree
by
Kandice E. Geddes

What do you do when you and your twin sister are attracted to the same man?

Fight it out of course...

Or there's always the nicer option of helping your much quieter sister catch the guy.

Identical twins, Paige and Pam, have been inseparable their whole lives. Paige is outgoing and bubbly, whereas Pam is quiet and insecure. They share everything from clothes, to shoes, to the peaches in their family's orchard. But when it comes to men, Pam has always backed down. Unfortunately, they have the same taste as far as the male species goes as well.

But this time, Paige feels like it's her sisterly duty to help Pam catch the guy, even if Chase Spencer is likely the most attractive man to walk the face of the planet. He's tall, dark, and has the dreamiest blue eyes Paige has ever seen. But when she discovers how over the moon Pam is for him, she devises a plan to help her sister come out of her shell, coaching her in ways to attract a man, even if that involves pretending to be Pam when the need calls for it.

Too bad in all her attempts to help her sister, Paige has fallen even harder for Chase, and even worse, he seems to have fallen hard for her as well, thinking she's her twin. Now she's torn between telling Chase and Pam the truth and risk losing both of their trust forever, or keeping her secret going while hoping everything somehow works out. Yeah, not likely…

Oh, the webs we weave…

The Journey Home

The Last First Kiss

Ready to Soar

Love in the Looking Glass

Magic in the Rain

ABOUT THE AUTHOR

Award winning and best-selling author Lucinda Race is a lifelong fan of romantic fiction. As a girl, she spent hours reading and dreaming of one day becoming a writer. As her life twisted and turned, she found herself writing nonfiction articles, but longed to turn to her true passion: novels. After developing the storyline for the Loudon Series, it was time to start living her dream.
Lucinda lives with her husband Rick and two little pups, Jasper and Griffin, in the rolling hills of Western Massachusetts. Her writing is contemporary, fresh, and engaging.
Visit her at:
www.facebook.com/lucindaraceauthor
Twitter @lucindarace
Instagram @lucindaraceauthor
www.lucindarace.com
Lucinda@lucindarace.com